ROBERT B. PARKER'S
KILLING THE BLUES

This Large Print Book carries the
Seal of Approval of N.A.V.H.

A JESSE STONE NOVEL

Robert B. Parker's Killing the Blues

Michael Brandman

LARGE PRINT PRESS
A part of Gale, Cengage Learning

GALE
CENGAGE Learning·

Detroit • New York • San Francisco • New Haven, Conn • Waterville, Maine • London

GALE
CENGAGE Learning®

LIBRARY OF CONGRESS CATALOGING-IN-PUBLICATION DATA

Brandman, Michael.
  Robert B. Parker's Killing the blues : a Jesse Stone novel / by Michael Brandman.
    p. cm. — (Thorndike Press large print core)
    ISBN-13: 978-1-4104-4052-5 (hardcover)
    ISBN-10: 1-4104-4052-4 (hardcover)
    1. Stone, Jesse (Fictitious character)—Fiction. 2. City and town life—Massachusetts—Fiction. 3. Police chiefs—Massachusetts—Fiction. 4. Large type books. I. Parker, Robert B., 1932–2010. II. Title. III. Title: Killing the blues.
  PS3602.R356R63 2011b
  813'.6—dc22   2011029513

ISBN 13: 978-1-59413-562-0 (pbk. : alk. paper)
ISBN 10: 1-59413-562-2 (pbk. : alk. paper)

Published in 2012 by arrangement with G. P. Putnam's Sons, a member of Penguin Group (USA) Inc.

Printed in the United States of America
  1 2 3 4 5   16 15 14 13 12

FD254

For Joanna . . .
. . . who makes everything possible . . .
. . . and for Bob

1

Coffee was the only thing on Jesse Stone's mind when he entered the Paradise police station on a bright New England spring morning.

His first stop was usually the coffeemaker. But when he saw what was happening in front of Suitcase Simpson's desk, which was located across the aisle from the kitchen area, he headed for his office.

A man and a woman, middle-aged, expensively dressed, and handsomely coiffed, were arguing loudly with Suitcase. The man was irate. His face was beet-red, and the woman was obviously concerned for him.

"Molly," he said, "what's going on?"

She followed him into his office.

"Tourists. Missing vehicle. They exited the turnpike at Paradise Road, looking for a place to have breakfast. They discovered Daisy's. Sometime while they were eating, their car disappeared. Late-model Honda Civic."

"What's with the yelling," Jesse said.

"They believe the car was towed."

"And they think we towed it?"

"Yes. Because it was parked illegally."

"You mean they didn't park in Daisy's lot?"

"Correct."

"And did they say why they didn't park in Daisy's lot?"

"When they chose Daisy's, they weren't certain they were gonna like it. So they parked on the street. In a red zone. When they decided it was okay, they never went back to move the car."

"And that's why they think it was towed?"

"Yes."

"Was it?"

"Rich is checking on that as we speak."

Jesse sighed.

"Molly, can I ask you a question?"

"Since when do you need permission to ask me a question," she said.

"May I have a cup of coffee, please?"

"You may. There's some fresh."

"I know. I can smell it."

"Do you want me to wait here while you get it?"

"I want you to get it for me."

"You want me to get coffee for you?"

"Yes."

She gave him the look.

"I don't want to have to deal with those people just yet," Jesse said.

"Because?"

"Because I'm the decider, and I have decided that I don't want to deal with those people just yet. Will you please get me a cup of coffee?"

"You're gonna owe me for this, Jesse," Molly said, as she left the office.

It's never easy, Jesse thought.

Molly returned with the coffee, followed by Suitcase and the couple from the hall.

"They wanted to speak with you directly," Molly said, as she handed Jesse the cup.

The couple pushed past Molly and stood directly in front of Jesse's desk.

"What are you doing about our car," the man said.

"Jesse Stone," Jesse said. "I'm the chief of police here."

"Norman Steinberg," the man said. "My wife, Linda. We want to know what you're doing about our car."

"Suit," Jesse said. "What have we learned from Bauer?"

"He's at Smitty's Towing now, Jesse," Suitcase said.

"And?"

"He hasn't located it."

9

"You mean it's not there?"

"Looks like it, Jesse."

"Could it be possible that the car was stolen?" Jesse said.

The phone rang, and Molly answered it.

"It's Bauer," she said to Jesse. "He wants to talk to you."

Jesse picked up the phone.

"What have we got, Rich," he said.

"We got a problem, Skipper," Bauer said. "Not only is the Steinberg Honda not at Smitty's, but there's a woman here looking for her car, claiming that it, too, has gone missing. And the funny part is her car is also a Honda."

When things had finally calmed down and the Steinbergs had been taken to Paradise Car Rental, Jesse sat quietly, thinking.

Today was moving day for him. He had finally acted on his wish to move out of the condo where he'd lived since coming to Paradise.

He had rented it when he first arrived, when his future was uncertain. Despite its view of the harbor, it was basically a utilitarian space that had served his needs at the time.

But as the years went by and his position in Paradise became more secure, he began

10

to yearn for something more suited to his personality and his desire for privacy.

It was Captain Healy, the state homicide commander and a resident of Paradise, who had called Jesse's attention to the small house situated on an inlet, not far from Paradise Cove. It was two stories, barely more than a cottage, positioned on a bluff overlooking the bay. Its weathered appearance and remoteness made it feel both mysterious and enticing.

It was owned by an elderly physician and his wife who decided they had finally lived through enough New England winters. They were moving to Florida to be near their children and grandchildren and away from the cold.

But they couldn't bear to sell it. Their life had been in Paradise; their children had been born there.

The possibility existed that they might miss it too much and decide to return. As an interim step, they opted to rent it.

Healy knew the couple and made the introductions. He thought they would find security entrusting their home to the Paradise police chief.

It was well within Jesse's price range, partially furnished, and isolated enough to be attractive to him. Despite the inconvenience of having to lug his groceries across the narrow footbridge that spanned the bay, he fell in love with the place at first sight.

What little furniture he owned would be handled by Dexter's Movers. He had boxed and packed his few belongings and his clothing. Dexter's would move it all.

Jesse had taken one final tour of the condo. Not sentimental by nature, he still had feelings for it, and as he prepared to leave it for the last time, he felt a momentary pang of uncertainty.

Then he'd thought better of it and turned the key in at the management office. He bid the condo good-bye.

His thoughts returned to the missing vehicles.

Only idiots and dead men believe in coincidence, he remembered having read somewhere. It wasn't likely that the disappearance of two Hondas on the same day in the same town could be unrelated.

His first thought was that the cars had been stolen. He knew that gang-related automobile thefts often took place in New England, but they had never before occurred in Paradise.

The summer season was about to begin, and the last thing Jesse wanted to see in his office was the faces of tourists whose vehicles had disappeared.

And although he cared little for him, Jesse was certain the same would hold true for Carter Hansen, the current head of the Paradise Board of Selectmen.

As he left his office, Jesse could hear the sound of warning bells tolling ominously in his brain.

2

Carter Hansen waited for Jesse to enter the meeting hall before bringing the annual State of the Summer in Paradise conference to order.

As was his custom, Jesse took a seat in the back row, alongside Molly and Suitcase.

Today's conference had attracted a good-sized audience, comprised mostly of town luminaries and interested citizens.

Most of the regular Paradise police officers were there. Peter Perkins. Arthur Angstrom. Richard Bauer. There were a few of the new summer hires as well.

The five members of the board of selectmen were seated on the dais, including the newly reelected Hastings Hathaway, once the head selectman.

Hasty had owned the First City Bank of Paradise. Facing possible failure, however, he had aligned himself with a Boston-based mobster and had begun using the bank to launder money, a career that abruptly ended when his crimes were discovered by Jesse Stone, whom Hasty himself had hired.

He was apprehended, tried, and sentenced to five years in prison, a sentence that was later reduced to two years. With time off for good behavior, Hasty wound up serving only sixteen months.

Upon his release, having been legally barred from returning to the world of banking, Hasty opened an upscale used car dealership.

His infectious ebullience and easy charm contributed to his success, and when he sought reelection to the board, running on a "redemption" platform, he won handily.

Carter Hansen, who had become the head selectman by default when Hasty had gone to jail, was none too happy to welcome him back. He believed that the board of selectmen was no place for a convicted felon. Hansen was also unhappy that years ago, against his better judgment, Hasty had hired Jesse Stone.

Although Hansen was forced to admit that Chief Stone turned out to be an effective lawman, there was no love lost between them.

He gaveled the meeting to order.

"Citizens of Paradise," he said, pleased

with the sound of his voice. "This meeting will now come to order. The summer season is once again upon us, and there is much to be done."

His gaze settled on Jesse.

"Chief Stone, have you anything you want to tell us regarding your plans for the summer?"

Jesse remained seated and silent, creating a moment of discomfort for Hansen. Finally, he stood and spoke.

"We're ready," he said.

Then he sat back down.

"That's it," Hansen said. "That's all you have to say?"

Jesse nodded.

On the dais, Selectman Morris Comden leaned over to snicker in Hansen's ear.

"Not too much of a talker, is he?"

Hansen ignored the remark.

"For the record, Chief Stone, let it be known that the board of selectmen has approved funding for the hiring of additional law enforcement personnel for the summer season. This will give us a greater capability in the service of tourism, which is Paradise's principal source of income. I assume this meets with your approval."

"It does," Jesse said.

"I assume that the force has been properly

instructed as to the acceptable rules of behavior for a long and arduous summer season."

"It has."

Jesse noticed that Molly was staring at him with a look of exasperation on her face.

He turned to her and grinned.

Carter Hansen sat silently.

Jesse sat silently.

Finally, Hansen spoke.

"All right, then," he said. "Now that we've heard from Chief Stone, I'd like to introduce Alexis Richardson, who has been hired to head the public-relations and event-planning campaign for the upcoming season. It will be up to Alexis to spread the word that Paradise is *the* hot new location for summer tourism."

Jesse watched as a young woman in the front row stood and, amid a scattering of applause, made her way to the lectern.

He listened attentively as she discussed her plans to create a summer music festival. She looked to be in her late twenties, exceptionally pretty and fashionably slender. She wore a black Donna Karan summer suit with a very short skirt and a white open-collared blouse. A simple gold chain adorned her neck. Her pale skin was complemented by expertly styled shoulder-length jet-black hair, which she constantly brushed from her forehead with a swipe of her hand.

As she spoke, her eyes scanned the audience, stopping occasionally on Jesse. Her talk was short, and afterward she returned to her seat.

Carter Hansen took to the lectern and talked briefly before calling on a handful of prominent business leaders, the CEO of Paradise Memorial Hospital, the fire captain, and the head of the Sanitation Department.

As was the case with Ms. Richardson, each of the speakers devoted their remarks to their own summer initiatives and their varying degrees of readiness.

Jesse's attention waned.

His thoughts turned to Sunny Randall. Although they had decided to take the next step in their somewhat quixotic relationship, things had suddenly changed when she accepted a job that took her to Europe for the summer.

Once she had gone, he began to feel the weight of his commitment easing. He began to have doubts. He was haunted by remembrances of his marriage to Jenn. He felt his psychic defenses reestablishing themselves. He found himself becoming more and more reclusive and increasingly secure in his solitude.

He was suddenly wrenched from his reverie.

"Jesse," Molly said, "wake up. The meeting's over."

3

When Jesse and Molly left the Town Hall, they found clusters of people milling about on the sidewalk, talking in small groups.

Alexis Richardson stood alone, her eyes searching the crowd.

"Chief Stone," she said, when she spotted Jesse.

She approached him.

"Jesse," he said.

He liked the way she looked. Even more so up close.

"Alexis," she said. "Do you think you could make some time for me, Jesse? I'd like to stop by and share my thoughts about the summer with you."

Jesse didn't say anything.

She moved closer to him and lowered her voice.

"I have some ideas about how to success-fully promote tourism," she said. "I sub-scribe to the spring-break theory. All-day music festivals. Rock and roll. They'll swarm to Paradise like they did to Woodstock. They'll be sleeping fifteen deep on the beach."

"There's no sleeping on the beach," Jesse said.

"I'm very serious about this, Jesse," she said.

Hasty Hathaway approached them.

"Jesse," he said.

"Hasty," Jesse said.

Alexis took the moment to make her getaway. Looking at Jesse, she lifted her hand to her ear, thumb and pinky extended as if she was holding a telephone, and silently mouthed the words *I'll call you.*

"I hope I didn't interrupt anything," Hasty said, as he watched her walk away. "That girl has some pair of legs on her."

"I'm glad to see that some things don't change, Hasty," Jesse said.

"What's this about a car or two going missing," Hasty said. "I heard a couple of Hondas disappeared."

"Don't believe everything you hear."

"It's a small town, Jesse. Things don't stay secret for very long."

Jesse didn't say anything.

"If you ever need anything," Hasty said.

"Anything at all, you'll be sure to let me know?"

"I will."

"I hope you're not just saying that."

"I'm not just saying that, Hasty."

"I hope not," Hasty said. "You know, I'm very fond of you, Jesse."

Jesse placed his hand on Hasty's shoulder for a moment, then turned away.

He spotted Molly and walked toward her.

The sidewalk crowd had thinned. Several of the lingerers greeted Jesse as he passed.

"You running for office," Molly said.

"I'm a very popular figure here, Moll."

"That's only because you're the police chief."

"What are you saying?"

"What I'm saying is that your popularity is an illusion. Something that comes with the job. Try not to let it go to your head."

"I'm crushed."

"I know. You just stick with me. It's my job to keep you illusion-free."

"And it's a fine job that you're doing, too. Keep it up and there could be a big promotion in it for you."

"Promotion to what," Molly said.

"Let me get back to you on that," Jesse said. They began walking toward Jesse's cruiser.

"You know something, Moll," Jesse said.

"What?"

"I think we might just have our hands full with Ms. Richardson."

"In what way," Molly said.

"Rock and roll," Jesse said.

"Which means?"

"Trouble. Right here in River City."

4

It was early evening, and Jesse had already made several trips across the footbridge, each time carrying armloads of groceries and supplies.

He strolled through the rooms of the small house, stepping around his boxes, acknowledging the existing furniture and trying to determine where he'd place his own.

He walked onto the back porch, which overlooked the bay. He breathed in the crisp night air. The remoteness of the house offered a level of privacy and quiet that had escaped him when he lived in the condo.

He went back upstairs. He scanned the boxes in search of the one marked "linens." He found his sheets and pillowcases and proceeded to make up his bed.

He had just stepped out of the shower when he realized that someone was knocking loudly on his front door.

"Hold on," Jesse said. "I'm coming."

He dried himself off as best he could and wrapped the towel around his waist. With water still dripping from his hair, he opened the door.

Healy, now his neighbor, stood before him.

"Have I come at a bad time," he said.

"What makes you say that," Jesse said.

"I was on my way home, so I thought I'd stop by to see how you were doing," Healy said. "So how are you doing?"

Jesse was not yet completely dry. His towel had come loose, and he only just managed to grab it before it fell to the floor.

"Your fly is open," Healy said.

Jesse stared at him.

"Would it be too much trouble if I asked you to entertain yourself while I tend to my dishabille?"

"Your dishabille," Healy said.

"My clothing," Jesse said. "A simple translation for the benefit of any dolts who might be standing in my doorway."

"Go right ahead," Healy said. "Where do you keep the scotch?"

"In the kitchen," Jesse said, as he started up the stairs.

Healy went inside, found the bottle, and helped himself to a healthy pour of Jesse's Johnny Black.

He opened the two French doors that led from the living room to the porch. He went outside.

Haphazardly placed on the porch were a love seat, a couple of tables, and a pressed-wood armchair, none of which appeared to have ever been new.

Healy sat down on the armchair, content to sip his scotch and stare silently at the sparkling reflection of the setting sun on the restless waters of the bay.

Jesse, dressed in jeans and a sweater, joined him. He carried a scotch of his own.

"Beautiful out here," Healy said.

Jesse nodded and sat down on the love seat.

"Thanks for this," Jesse said. "It already feels like home."

Healy smiled.

"It's a great house," he said.

Jesse smiled.

They sat quietly for a while.

"I gather you lost a couple of Hondas," Healy said.

"I wonder if there's anyone in Massachusetts who hasn't heard about those Hondas," Jesse said.

"This might not be an isolated incident," Healy said. "My guys are noticing higher-than-usual incidents of car theft. The

26

organized-crime unit thinks this might be the start of something."

"Something Mob-related?"

"Yes."

"In Paradise?"

"They think so," Healy said.

"Do the OC guys think that our friends in the underworld are organizing chop shops in Paradise?"

"We're hearing that your so-called friends are sensing enormous potential in doing business in this neck of the woods," Healy said.

Jesse didn't say anything.

"Summer in particular appeals to them," Healy said. "Large number of tourists. Lots of vehicles. They can slip in, snatch a car, strip it, chop it, and get rid of it in virtually no time."

"Hondas and Toyotas," Jesse said.

"Easiest to move," Healy said.

"Lucrative," Jesse said.

"Breathtakingly so," Healy said.

"Any thoughts on how to stop them," Jesse said.

"I'm with Homicide, not the Registry of Motor Vehicles."

"There must be a connection."

"When you find one, you'll be certain to let me know," Healy said.

27

"A fine way to start the season," Jesse said.

"It could be worse," Healy said.

"How?"

"It could be drugs."

"That would be worse," Jesse said. "Any idea who's running the operation?"

"We're still working on that."

"So was this the reason for your visit?"

"This and a sincere interest in your personal well-being."

"Sincerity hasn't always been your strongest suit."

"But at least I'm working on it," Healy said.

"Try not to hurt yourself," Jesse said.

They sat quietly on the porch, sipping their scotch, watching the sun slip lower over the horizon, appearing and disappearing amid the gathering clouds of evening.

It was Healy who broke the silence.

"There's a cat sitting over there by the bushes."

"Where?"

"There. Black and white. Scrawny-looking. Yours?"

"Not mine," Jesse said.

Healy finished his scotch.

"I gotta go," he said. "You'll let me know if this car thing escalates?"

"You have my word on it," Jesse said.

"Goody," Healy said.

Jesse walked him to the door.

"Thanks for the heads-up," Jesse said.

"Thanks for the scotch," Healy said.

Jesse walked with Healy to the footbridge.

"You gotta carry your groceries across it," Healy said.

"I do if I want to eat," Jesse said.

"I don't envy you that," Healy said.

"Me either," Jesse said.

After Healy left, Jesse washed the glasses, dried them and put them away.

Then he went back outside to look for the cat.

5

The cat reappeared the next morning. Jesse spotted it as he gazed idly out the French doors while setting up his telephone answering machine.

It was sitting by the bushes that bordered Jesse's yard.

It was indeed black and white, but the fur on its face appeared to have been distributed comically. Above the nose it was black; below it, white. The fur on its back was black, but its stomach was white. This distinctive coloration rendered the impression that the cat might very well have been wearing a tuxedo and a mask.

It was scrawny, as Healy had observed. Hungry, too. When it saw Jesse through the window, it mewed loudly.

Jesse went into the kitchen and scrounged up his one can of tuna fish. He opened it and scraped the contents into a bowl, which he then carried outside.

The cat eyed him warily from the bushes.

Jesse placed the bowl on the deck. Then he went back inside and closed the doors. He watched to see what the cat would do next.

After several moments, it stood up and stretched itself languorously. Then it suddenly sat back down and began to vigorously lick one of its paws. It stood up again and began to inch its way toward the house.

The cat stopped inching when it reached the top step of the porch. There it sat down, all the while keeping its eyes on both the door and the bowl.

It stayed that way for several minutes.

Satisfied that no one was lying in wait, the cat sidled up to the bowl.

At first it only sniffed the tuna. Then it licked it. Then it tentatively picked up a morsel and, after dropping it on the deck, crouched down and ate it.

Following a brief moment of indecision, it returned to the bowl and gobbled the rest.

Jesse smiled.

He left the house and went to work.

It was late afternoon when Molly called out to Jesse that Captain Cronjager, his old boss from the LAPD, was on line one.

He couldn't imagine why Cronjager would

be calling him. They hadn't spoken since the captain had phoned to congratulate him on getting the job in Paradise. Which had been years ago.

When he picked up the call, he was greeted with Cronjager's familiar sandpaper gargle.

"Stone," he said. "How the hell are you?"

"Better since I gave up hope," Jesse said.

Cronjager laughed heartily.

"To what do I owe the honor," Jesse said.

"Do you remember a dickhead called Rollo Nurse," Cronjager said.

"Remind me," Jesse said.

"He was the lughead you busted during a botched robbery attempt just before I shit-canned you."

"Eloquently stated," Jesse said.

"In case your memory needs jarring, you weren't having one of your better days when you busted this guy. You managed to rough him up pretty good."

"I roughed up a lot of guys pretty good when I worked for you."

"Yeah, well, I thought you might like to know that this particular dirtbag got out of Lompoc on an early-release program. Seems that California is going broke, and the governor chose to spit out a fair-sized portion of the prison population in the interest of saving the state some dough. Rollo Nurse was one of them."

"And you're telling me this because . . ." Jesse said.

"Given what you did to him, he probably hasn't forgotten. And now he's out. One of the Lompoc bulls thinks he's gone unhinged. We think he's the type who might come looking for you."

"And what makes you think he would know how to find me," Jesse said.

"If he can work a computer, he could find you," Cronjager said.

"How?" Jesse said.

"He could Google you," Cronjager said. "I did it myself."

"Google me," Jesse said.

"Yep," Cronjager said.

"Shit," Jesse said.

"Yeah," Cronjager said.

"Google," Jesse said. "What does it say?"

"It lists you. Jesse Stone, Chief of Police, Paradise, Mass."

"Whatever happened to privacy," Jesse said.

"It went the way of the Pontiac," Cronjager said. "He knows where you are."

"Or not," Jesse said.

"Or not," Cronjager said. "In any event, forewarned is whatever the hell it is."

"Thanks for this, Captain," Jesse said.

"Don't mention it, big guy. Healy tells me you're doing good out there. I'm happy for you."

Then the line went dead as Cronjager ended the call. Jesse sat quietly for a while.

"Rich Bauer on line one," Molly said, calling out to Jesse from her desk.

Jesse picked up the call.

"What's up, Rich," Jesse said.

"We got another one, Skipper. This one's bad."

6

Jesse, with Suitcase beside him, spotted the flashing lights of Rich Bauer's Crown Vic as he pulled his cruiser into the Cineplex parking lot. A Paradise General ambulance was parked alongside Bauer's cruiser. As they approached, Jesse told Suit to immediately institute containment procedures and to call for backup.

Bauer was standing alongside his vehicle. The door was open. A woman was seated inside, visibly shaken. The body of a man lay on the pavement before them. Two EMTs stood next to the body.

Jesse motioned for Bauer to join him. "What's happening here?" he said.

"The woman and her husband were leaving the theater when they encountered someone attempting to steal their car. The husband confronted the guy, who then got out of the car and attacked him. Killed him."

Jesse looked at the body. The man's neck lay at an odd angle, obviously broken.

One of the EMTs looked back at Jesse and shook his head.

"Did you call Mel Snyderman," Jesse said to Bauer.

"The ME?"

Jesse nodded.

"Not yet," Bauer said.

"You might want to give him a call. Fill him in on what happened."

"Will do, Skipper," Bauer said.

"You might also want to cover the body," Jesse said.

"Sure thing, Skipper," Bauer said. "I'll get right on it."

Jesse approached the woman, who was sitting quietly, staring blankly ahead.

"Jesse Stone," he said. "Paradise police chief."

The woman looked up at him.

"Can you tell me what took place here, Mrs. . . ."

"Lytell," she said. "Nancy Lytell."

"Can you tell me what happened, Mrs. Lytell?"

"Mike and I were at a movie," she said. "We didn't much care for it, so we left early. We saw this person inside our car. Mike, he always had a short fuse on him. He ran to the car and said something. I couldn't hear. Then . . ."

Jesse waited.

"The man got out of the car and pushed Mike. He grabbed him and lifted him up. Then he threw him against the car."

The parking lot filled with the sound of sirens as two police cruisers arrived.

"What happened then," Jesse said.

"I don't know. Mike was on the ground. He wasn't moving. The man got back in the car. He somehow managed to get it started, and he drove away."

"Can you describe the suspect?"

"The suspect?"

"The man who attacked your husband. Can you remember what he looked like?"

"I'm not really certain. He was bigger than Mike. It all happened so fast. I can't really remember."

"What type of vehicle was it," Jesse said.

"What type?"

"What make."

"Oh. It was a Honda. An Accord."

Jesse didn't say anything.

"I had my cell phone, you know. I used it to call nine-one-one. I sat next to Mike until that policeman arrived. Is he . . ."

"Your husband has passed away, Mrs. Lytell," Jesse said. "I'm sorry."

The woman sat silently for a while. "I knew it," she said.

She started to cry.

Jesse summoned Bauer and told him to remain with the woman. Jesse asked him to try to locate a relative or a friend, someone who could stay with her.

Then he went to talk with Suitcase and the other officers who had responded to the call.

"I want the site cordoned. Shield the body. Keep people moving. No gawkers. I want this kept quiet. No press. Mel Snyderman and his crew should be here shortly."

"What do you make of this," Suit said.

"Nothing good," Jesse said.

It was dark when Jesse got home.

Even in the dark, he loved the house. The night sounds and shadows lent it an aura of mystery. He could see the stars clearly. He could hear and smell the ocean outside.

He went inside and placed the bag of groceries on the kitchen counter. He placed his Colt Combat Commander on it also. He put some ice in a glass and poured himself a scotch. He drank some.

He turned the porch lights on and went outside to look for the cat. He couldn't see it. He went inside and unpacked the groceries. He pulled out a bag of dry cat food and a dozen cans of wet food.

He took a bowl from the shelf, and got a half-gallon jug of milk from the refrigerator. He brought them both outside. He placed the bowl on the deck and filled it with milk.

He went back to the kitchen and filled another bowl with dry food, which he took outside and placed next to the milk.

Then he went inside.

He finished his scotch and poured himself another. He sat down in front of the TV with his take-out turkey burger and fries.

He turned on the old-movie channel and watched a bit of the Marx Brothers in *Horse Feathers.* He admired Harpo's ability to always remain silent.

Afterward he went back outside. Although the cat remained unseen, Jesse noticed that the dry food had been eaten and most of the milk was gone.

He turned off the porch lights and poured himself another scotch. He took note of the fact that it was his third of the night. The scotch hadn't erased the look in Mrs. Lytell's eyes, which continued to haunt him. He poured himself another.

He stopped short of drinking it, however. He knew he was on the edge. He put the glass down, climbed the stairs, and went to bed.

7

"So that's why you phoned me," Dix said.

"Yes," Jesse said.

Jesse sat back in the chair opposite Dix, who was drinking a mug of coffee.

"Because you almost got wasted?"

"Yes."

"And you almost got wasted because . . . ?"

"Something about the look in that woman's eyes. They seemed so violated."

"Was there anything else?"

"The phone call."

"You were upset by Cronjager's call?"

"I might have been."

"And you wanted to discuss it with me."

"Yes."

"If we're gonna get anywhere, you'll have to stop giving me one-word answers," Dix said.

"You're asking questions that only require one-word answers."

"Is this gonna be as hard as I think it'll be?"

"Maybe," Jesse said.

"Okay. What exactly was it about Cronjager's call that upset you?"

"When I took down this Rollo Nurse character, I was in terrible shape. Jenn was fucking Elliot. I had moved out of my house. I was drinking heavily."

"And?"

"And I took it out on Rollo Nurse."

"You hurt him."

"Badly. Don't get me wrong. He was an arrogant son of a bitch. I didn't like him. At first sight I didn't like him. So when he gave me all this attitude and refused to obey my commands, I decked him."

"With your fist?"

"With my fist and the butt end of my pistol."

"You mean you hit him in the head with your pistol," Dix said.

"Yes."

"More than once?"

"Three times. I'm pretty certain that I fractured his skull."

Dix didn't say anything.

"I did fracture his skull, okay? I could hear it. I can still hear it. I was wasted, and I exercised no restraint."

"What did the doctors say?"

"That he might not fully recover. That he might suffer residual damage."

"Such as," Dix said.

"Headaches. Lapses in memory. Dementia."

"How did that make you feel?"

"At the time, I felt nothing. Later, I began to feel guilty," Jesse said.

"Guilty for?"

"For wasting some piece of detritus who perhaps deserved better."

"And if you had it to do all over again?"

"I'm afraid that if he shows up here and starts acting cute, I might have to kill him."

"And you want me to do what for you," Dix said.

"Help me to exercise restraint."

"Because?"

"Because I'm not certain I'll be able to control myself."

"Because?"

"Because he's a shitbag."

Dix didn't say anything.

"Despite the fact that I hurt him and that my reasons for hurting him were more related to my own issues than to his, it worries me that this thing still isn't over and that in all likelihood I'm gonna have to kill him."

"And," Dix said.

"And in an odd way, I'm looking forward to it."

8

Suitcase was waiting when Jesse pulled his cruiser to a stop in front of the station.

"Get in," Jesse said.

Suitcase did, and they pulled away from the curb.

"Anything on the killing," Suit said.

"Nothing."

"Where are we going?"

"On a training mission," Jesse said.

"A training mission?"

"Police work isn't all fun and games, Suit. A good cop needs to be properly trained. I took a number of classes before I qualified for the LAPD."

"I only took one," Suit said.

"Which is why it's important that you listen and learn. I want you involved in this car theft business."

"I thought Rich Bauer was involved in it."

"He was," Jesse said.

"What do you mean?"

"I mean that I want him less involved."

"Because?"

"Because he's a nitwit."

Suitcase didn't say anything.

"And he tries my patience."

Suitcase still didn't say anything.

"I want you on this, Suit."

"So you think it will escalate?"

"I know it will."

"How do you know?"

"Coply intuition," Jesse said.

He pulled to a stop in a no-parking zone directly in front of the Town Hall. They got out of the car and went inside.

Carter Hansen was standing in front of his office when Jesse and Suitcase arrived.

"So now we have a killing on our hands," Hansen said.

"Why don't we dispense with the niceties and get right down to business," Jesse said.

"I'm not a big fan of your sarcasm, Stone," Hansen said. "What are you going to do?"

Hansen ushered them into his office and sat down at his desk. Jesse and Suitcase sat opposite him.

"We'd love some," Jesse said.

"Excuse me," Hansen said.

"Coffee. We'd love some," Jesse said.

After a moment, Hansen picked up the phone and dialed a number.

"Marilyn, would you please bring some coffee for Chief Stone and Officer Simpson."

He hung up the phone.

"What are you doing about this killing, Stone," Hansen said.

"Jesse," Jesse said. "I much prefer Jesse."

Hansen glared at him.

"I need you to purchase a couple of vehicles," Jesse said.

"You need me to do what?"

"I need two vehicles. Both Hondas. One Civic. One Accord. Used."

"May I ask what for," Hansen said.

"I'm going to use them as bait."

"This has something to do with the car thefts," Hansen said.

"It does," Jesse said.

"Do you believe that the killing and the car thefts are related?"

Jesse didn't say anything.

The door to Hansen's office opened, and a middle-aged woman entered carrying a tray filled with two cups of coffee, a small pitcher of milk, and a handful of sugar packets. She placed it on the sideboard, smiled at the two officers and left.

"Are you planning to catch them by using these vehicles," Hansen said.

"Not exactly," Jesse said, sipping his coffee.

"Then what are you planning to do?"

"I'm not going to tell you."

"You're not going to tell me?"

"That's correct," Jesse said. "How do I go about requisitioning the Hondas?"

"Now, wait just a minute," Hansen said. "Why do you think that the board of selectmen would purchase these vehicles without knowing what you're planning to do with them?"

"Because I'm the police chief."

"Well, I won't," Hansen said.

Jesse sat silently.

Suitcase sat silently.

Hansen sat silently.

Finally, Jesse broke the silence.

"You're going to purchase these vehicles because you have no wish to see car theft and murder destroy the summer season," he said. "If the media were to connect this killing to our current crime wave, you can just imagine how that story would play. You might as well post a 'town closed for the summer' sign in front of the speed trap."

Hansen continued to sit silently.

Finally, he said, "Have the dealership send the bill to me directly. And in the future,

Chief Stone, please refer to it as the entrance to Paradise, not the speed trap."

9

Jesse parked the cruiser in front of Hathaway's Previously Owned Quality Vehicles. The building had once been home to a Saturn dealership, but when General Motors pulled the plug, Hasty bought it for what he referred to as "chump change."

Jesse and Suitcase walked through the showroom and knocked on the door to Hasty's office, which was open.

"It's open," Hasty said.

They entered the office. Hasty looked up at them.

"Am I being arrested," he said.

"I want to buy a couple of used Hondas," Jesse said, as he and Suitcase sat down.

"Hondas," Hasty said. "Forget Hondas. Let me set you up with an outstanding pair of Lincolns."

"Forget the sales pitch, Hasty," Jesse said. "Hondas. Vintage 2005, give or take. Two of 'em."

"What do you want with two Hondas," Hasty said. "Is this related to those car thefts?"

"None of your business," Jesse said. "Do you have the Hondas, or do I have to go to O'Brien's?"

"Is he always this personable," Hasty said to Suitcase.

Suitcase smiled.

"I don't have them in stock," Hasty said. "Give me a day or two. I'll get them. Who's paying, by the way?"

"Board of selectmen," Jesse said.

"I knew it was related to the car thefts."

"How much," Jesse said.

"Well," Hasty said, "seeing as how I have to import them, they're not gonna be cheap."

"Come on, Suit," Jesse said, as he stood up. "We're going to O'Brien's."

"Okay, okay," Hasty said. "Sit down. Sit down. I'll discount them."

"Hasty, these cars are for official business. I'm not here to play footsie with you over the price. I'll buy them from you only if you'll undersell the market," Jesse said. "And the transaction needs to remain confidential. No blabbing."

"Blabbing. You think I'd blab about this," Hasty said.

51

"All over town."

"You disappoint me, Jesse."

"Cut the crap, Hasty. Just get the two cars. You have until noon tomorrow. The bill goes directly to Carter Hansen."

Jesse and Suitcase started to leave.

"I wish I could say it was a pleasure doing business with you," Hasty said.

"Noon," Jesse said.

10

The big Greyhound bus pulled off the highway and into the Sun West Service Center just outside Topeka, Kansas. The driver brought it to a stop in front of the Trail's End Restaurant & Gift Shoppe and announced to the passengers that the rest period would last for ninety minutes.

Rollo Nurse climbed out of his seat at the rear of the bus, wrestled his shoulder bag from the overhead, and stepped outside.

He stretched and took a deep breath. The air was tangy with the odor of gasoline.

Rollo was tall. He stood six feet two but weighed barely a hundred and seventy-five pounds. He was a most unsightly man. The left side of his face drooped dramatically. His eyes were unbalanced, his mouth lopsided. He oozed unpleasantness.

He sat alone in the Trail's End Restaurant, eating a chicken-fried steak and muttering to himself under his breath.

He was thinking about the big cop from L.A. Rollo knew he had been wrong to challenge the cop by feigning ignorance of the crime. He knew he should have followed his instructions, but he hadn't. The cop reeked of booze, which had unsettled him.

The cop had hit him with his gun. Twice. In the head. He had attempted to surrender, only to be hit again.

He had gone down hard. He was dazed. His head had hurt terribly. The last thing he saw before he blacked out was the big cop standing over him, staring at him, dead-eyed.

He was put in a cell. Alone. Isolated. Over time, the pain receded. But now he had trouble remembering things. He had become vague and uncertain. He was damaged. The cop didn't have to hit him like that. Didn't have to hurt him so bad.

He was visited by dark voices that came in the night. They whispered rage. They filled his head with images of vengeance.

Then California's economy collapsed and he was suddenly free. With no parole restrictions.

Free to go where he wished. Free to do what he wished. Free to heed the dark voices.

The PA system in the restaurant blared

the announcement that the Greyhound bus to Boston was now boarding.

Rollo was first in line.

11

When Jesse and Suitcase returned to the station, they found Alexis Richardson sitting in the waiting area, reading a copy of Malcolm Gladwell's *Outliers: The Story of Success.*

She was wearing a colorful Missoni sweater over dark-rinse blue jeans. Her jet-black hair was pulled back in a sleek chignon. She wore a pair of horn-rimmed reading glasses. When she noticed Jesse, she looked up at him and smiled.

He invited her to join him in his office. She collected her things and went inside. Jesse exchanged a quick glance with Molly, then went inside himself.

"Thank you for seeing me without notice," Alexis said.

Jesse leaned back in his chair.

"May I ask you a question, Alexis?"

"That sounds ominous."

"It's just that I can't help but wonder how

a woman like yourself gets a job like this one."

"I studied public relations in college," she said. "Then I served an internship with a well-known event planner in New York."

"Where you actually planned events of your own," Jesse said.

"Not exactly."

When Jesse said nothing, she continued.

"The event planner gave me access and taught me the ropes."

"So how did you get this job?"

"I interviewed for it."

"You interviewed for it?"

"Yes."

"Who interviewed you?"

"Selectman Hansen."

"Carter Hansen interviewed you?"

"Yes."

"So he's the one who hired you."

"Yes."

"And that's how you met him?"

"No."

"No, that's not how you met him?"

"Yes."

"I'm confused," he said.

"Which part are you confused about," she said.

"The Hansen part. You didn't meet him on your job interview?"

"No."

"You met him prior to your job interview?"

"Yes."

"Alexis, the first rule of conversation is that you have to provide more than one-word answers."

"Selectman Hansen is my uncle," she said.

"Carter Hansen is your uncle," he said.

"My mother's brother," she said.

"So it was your uncle who hired you."

"Yes."

"Well, I'll be damned," Jesse said.

Alexis stood.

"Don't judge me, Jesse. I earned this job."

"I'm sure you did," he said. "What exactly did Hansen tell you about it?"

"Uncle Carter told me . . . I mean, Selectman Hansen told me that the board was interested in funding a handful of special events this summer, events designed to attract tourists."

"Rock-and-roll events?"

"Arts-based events. Not rock and roll."

"And he offered you the job of planning these events?"

"Yes."

"Was it your idea to introduce rock and roll into the mix?"

"No. Yes."

"Which is it?"

"I mentioned to Uncle Carter that a Woodstock-like event could reap amazing rewards."

"To which Uncle Carter replied?"

" 'We'll see.' "

"And have you made up your mind as to which events you'd like to present?"

"Yes."

"You want to tell me about them?"

"Yes."

"Here come those one-worders again."

"I want to begin with a rock festival. An all-day event. At the Paradise High School stadium."

"Funded by the board of selectmen?"

"Yes."

"Does Uncle Carter know?"

"Not yet."

"I'm flattered that you chose to tell me first," Jesse said. "When exactly were you planning on telling Uncle Carter?"

"Stop saying 'Uncle Carter.' "

"When were you planning on telling the selectman?"

"Soon."

"Soon would be good," Jesse said. They sat silently for a while.

"May I ask you a question, Jesse?"

"That sounds ominous."

"Would you consider having lunch?"

"Lunch?"

"With me."

"With you?"

"Yes."

"You mean now?"

Alexis laughed.

"Yes," she said.

Jesse didn't say anything.

"Have you anything better to do," she said.

He looked at her intently.

"Nothing I can think of," he said.

After agreeing to meet her at the juice bar in Nordmann's Fitness Center, Jesse began to pack up. As he left his office, he stopped by Molly's desk.

"Would you do me a favor, Moll," he said.

"That depends," she said.

"Will you please phone Captain Healy's office and ask if he could stop by my place on his way home this evening."

"Is it business or personal?"

"Excuse me?"

"Is it a business call or a personal call?"

"What difference does it make?"

"I'm not your social secretary, Jesse. I'm still reeling from the coffee incident."

"The coffee incident."

"You know what I'm talking about."

Their conversation had attracted the attention of Suitcase, who was seated at the desk next to Molly's. He was leaning forward in his chair, listening intently.

"You haven't answered my question," Molly said.

"What if I said it was a business call?"

"Then I'd most happily make it."

"And if I said it was personal?"

"Then you could make it yourself."

"Well, it's a business call."

"How do I know that?"

"Because I said so, that's how."

Molly didn't say anything.

"Have you always been such a hard case," Jesse said.

"Only since puberty," Molly said.

Jesse looked over at Suitcase, who quickly looked away.

"Am I wearing a 'kick me' sign or something," Jesse said, as he headed for the door. "Quit busting my chops and make the call, will you, please, Molly."

He left the building.

After he'd gone, Molly looked at Suitcase, and they both burst out laughing.

12

Like all of the new-wave fitness centers, Nordmann's was gigantic, football field–sized, containing every imaginable kind of electronic exercise machine. Jesse figured that if hyperactivity didn't pose the members a danger, the intensified electromagnetic field in which they exercised would more than likely neuter them.

He spotted Alexis Richardson among the treadmills. She waved to him. She was wearing tight blue leggings and a white tank top. Her hair was pulled back into a ponytail. She was jogging steadily on a treadmill that was running on high.

When she noticed Jesse, she slowed her jog, then turned off the machine but kept walking until it came to a stop. She stepped off and picked up her towel, patting her face before wrapping it around her neck.

"I'm a total fitness freak," she said. "Have been since I was a girl. You?"

"I was a baseball freak. Till I got hurt."

"You played baseball?"

"I did."

"Were you any good?"

"Triple-A good until I tore up my shoulder."

"So what do you do now?"

"I jog."

"Jogging is good."

"And I sulk."

They wandered over to the juice bar and ordered a couple of healthy-looking sandwiches. They sat at one of the tables.

"You do this a lot," Jesse said.

"Every day, if possible. I don't really feel right unless I've done at least two hours. I start with the treadmill and end up with the heavy bag."

"You work out on the heavy bag?"

"I do."

"You box?"

"Not exactly. I kickbox. I was on my college team. It's an artful sport. And there's nothing quite like the exhilaration of a lethal kick."

"You mean you've killed people?"

Alexis laughed.

"It's just an expression," she said.

They finished their lunch and she walked with Jesse to the door.

"Thank you," Alexis said. "It was lovely."

"Just like a first date," Jesse said. "Do you kiss and tell?"

"Don't tease me, Jesse. I like you."

"Ditto," he said.

Once home, Jesse stepped out of his clothes and into the shower. The steaming-hot water never failed to help ease the tensions of the day. He had just begun to feel better when he realized that someone was pounding on his door.

"Shit," he said.

Then he hollered, "All right."

He turned off the shower, dried himself the best he could, wrapped the towel around his waist, and gingerly made his sodden way to the kitchen, where he picked up his pistol. He press-checked it and went to the door.

It was Captain Healy.

"We have to stop meeting like this," Healy said.

Jesse stared at him.

Healy noticed Jesse's gun.

"Were you planning to shoot me," he said.

"You can't be too careful," Jesse said.

"Why don't you attend to your dishabille," Healy said. "I'll see myself in."

When Jesse returned, wearing jeans and a

sweater, he found Healy on the top step of the porch, holding a piece of Jesse's sliced chicken.

The black-and-white cat was standing directly in front of him, tentatively eating the chicken from his hand.

When Jesse stepped outside, the cat bolted. It leapt from the porch and dashed headlong into the bushes.

"I'm a cat person," Healy said. "Always have been. We currently have six. My wife calls me the Cat Whisperer."

"The Cat Whisperer," Jesse said.

"Unlikely, isn't it? I'm an anomaly."

"That's only the half of it."

"So what do you know," Healy said.

"Had to have been a newbie. Some low-life wannabe who came aboard when the operation expanded. Not a professional."

"Okay," Healy said.

"So he botches it. Dickwad thinks he's hit himself a home run. Gets rattled when the owner discovers him. Goes ballistic and kills the guy. Mob boys won't have been happy. Car theft isn't meant to be lethal."

"How do you know this?"

"It's what my gut tells me."

"What about the killer?"

"Most likely pushing up daisies in Paradise Gardens."

"So what are you gonna do?"

"I'm gonna run a break tomorrow. I've convinced Hansen to buy me a couple of Hondas. I'm gonna station them at critical locations and surveil them."

"And?"

"I'm gonna tail whoever shows up."

"Don't you mean 'whomever'?"

"Try not to parade your ignorance. I wanna spot them. See what happens."

"To what end?"

"Information-gathering. I don't really care about the small potatoes. What interests me is the big fish," Jesse said.

"Which reminds me, we're having snapper for dinner," Healy said. "I gotta go."

Once at the door, he turned back to Jesse.

"This could lead to some unpleasantness, Jesse," Healy said. "You're gonna want to be careful."

"I'm always careful."

"Like hell you are," Healy said.

After Healy had gone, Jesse went to the kitchen and got a couple of slices of chicken. He took them outside. He held a slice in his outstretched hand and called to the cat.

It didn't appear.

His arm began to tire. At last he placed the chicken on the step, stood up, and went inside.

"Cat Whisperer," he said.
He turned off the lights and went to bed.

13

Jesse collected the Hondas at noon. He brought Molly and Suitcase along, both of them in civilian clothing.

Suitcase drove the Accord directly to the police station and parked behind the building.

Molly drove the Civic to Paradise Mall, parking in a prearranged location. She got out of the car, made a show of gathering her belongings, then entered the mall.

She walked straight through and exited via a side door, where she was met by Rich Bauer. She got into his cruiser, and together they returned to the station.

The Civic remained where Molly had left it.

Three rows away, Peter Perkins sat low in the driver's seat of an unmarked Chevy, watching the Civic.

From a different vantage point, Jesse sat in his Ford Explorer, sipping coffee, also watching.

The hours passed and no one paid any attention to the Civic.

On cue, Peter Perkins drove away from the mall and was replaced by Arthur Angstrom, driving his Jeep Wrangler. Jesse remained in the Explorer.

When darkness began to settle, Bauer dropped Molly off at the mall. She backtracked through it on her way to the Civic, which she unlocked, got into, and drove away.

At the same time that Molly was leaving the mall, Suitcase was parking the Accord in front of the Cineplex Odeon Twelve. He got out of the car and went inside.

Arthur Angstrom drove his Wrangler past Suitcase just as he was entering the cinema. Angstrom parked several rows behind the Accord. He settled in to keep watch.

Jesse was parked nearby. He carefully unwrapped a meatball sandwich from Daisy's and ate it while he watched.

Nothing happened.

After all of the movies in the Cineplex had ended and the parking lot was emptying, Suitcase, Arthur, and Jesse each went their separate ways, calling it a night.

It was close to midnight when Jesse finally

got home, bone-tired.

He exercised caution before entering the house. Rollo Nurse caution, he deemed it. He carefully walked the perimeter. He determined that it hadn't been invaded. He opened the door and went inside.

"You can't be too careful these days," he said, to no one in particular.

He placed his gun on the kitchen counter, then went directly to the cupboard and took down a can of cat food. After emptying the contents into a bowl, he turned the porch lights on and stepped outside.

He picked up the empty bowl and re-placed it with the full one. He turned to go back inside but suddenly stopped.

Sitting on the love seat, staring at him, was the cat. Jesse stood frozen in his tracks.

"I'm Jesse," he said to the cat.

The cat didn't say anything.

"I'll just step inside now," Jesse said, as he walked gingerly toward the French doors.

Although it didn't attempt a getaway, the cat remained on alert.

Once inside, Jesse watched it jump off the love seat, saunter casually to the dish, crouch down, and eat.

Jesse smiled.

He forced himself to climb the stairs. He

lay down on the bed fully clothed. He was asleep the moment his head hit the pillow.

14

The Greyhound bus arrived in Boston on schedule. Rollo Nurse collected his things, stepped off the bus, and went inside the depot.

The Paradise bus wasn't scheduled to leave for another hour. Rollo bought a copy of the *Paradise Daily News* and sat down to study it. He leafed immediately to the "Rooms for Rent" section in the classifieds.

"Room to let in private home" caught his attention. "Walking distance to downtown. Nonsmoking. Clean. Quiet. Private bath. Contact Agatha Miller." It listed a number.

Rollo placed the call from one of the depot's decrepit phone booths. It was the voice of an older person that answered.

"Hello," she said.

"Is this Mrs. Miller?"

"This is Miss Miller."

"Miss Miller," Rollo said. "My name is Donald Johnson. I saw your ad in the paper.

Is the room still for rent?"

"It is still for rent. Yes."

"How much?"

"A hundred and twenty-five dollars per week. It also comes with a refrigerator."

"Can I see it?"

"What?"

"Can I see the room?"

"You may."

"Can I see it this afternoon? I could move in right away."

"You say you want to move in today?"

"Yeah."

"I see. What time were you thinking?"

"Around three o'clock."

"Very well, Mr. . . ."

"Johnson," Rollo said.

"Johnson. Yes. I forgot," Miss Miller said. "The address is Twenty-four Compton Street. I'll be awaiting your visit. Three o'clock."

"Yeah," Rollo said. He hung up.

The bus pulled into its slot in front of the Paradise Harbor Ferry Terminal. Rollo was the first to get off. He picked up his bag and went inside.

He bought a Paradise street map at the newsstand. He paid for it, got himself a coffee, and sat down to study the map.

73

He located Compton Street and traced the walking route from the terminal. He estimated he could make it in less than an hour. Although he would arrive earlier than expected, he set out immediately.

Compton turned out to be more of a lane than an actual street, barely wide enough to accommodate two cars. There were a total of six homes on Compton Street.

Two were grand-style New England Colonials, each set on acre-plus lots, each in pristine condition. There was a slightly run-down Cape Cod, a colorful split-level, and a pair of two-story Craftsman houses. The mature plantings and lush foliage lent the neighborhood a quaint, woodsy flavor.

The Miller house was one of the Craftsmans. It was carefully tended but weathered, sitting in the middle of a small lot. Rollo knocked on the door.

He heard the sound of footsteps, and then an elderly woman peered through the curtains.

"Yes," the woman said.

"Donald Johnson," Rollo said.

"Oh. Mr. Johnson. You're early." She opened the door.

"Yeah," he said.

The woman, who wore spectacles with thick lenses, gave Rollo the once-over.

Despite some misgivings regarding his unsightly appearance, she stood back and allowed him to enter.

"It's nice here," Rollo said.

"Thank you," she said. "I grew up in this house. My father built it himself."

"You live here alone?"

"Ever since my sister passed."

She showed Rollo to a small first-floor bedroom, situated at the rear of the house, at one time a maid's quarters. As advertised, it was clean, had a half-sized refrigerator and a small private bath.

She showed him the rest of the ground floor, explaining that the upstairs would be off-limits to him. He was, however, welcome to use the kitchen. He would also have use of the sitting room and TV. The backyard would be his to enjoy as well.

She asked if he might like to join her in a cup of tea.

As she stood filling the kettle, Rollo sat gazing at the kitchen with its paintings of dogs, decorative ceramic tiles, and colorful floral arrangements.

"You garden," he said.

"Why, yes. Yes, I do. Why do you ask?"

"I like flowers. These ones are very nice. Maybe you could put some in my room."

"That's certainly possible," she said.

"Yeah," he said. "I'd like that."

She served the tea. She placed a jar of honey on the table. She brought out a box of Social Tea biscuits. She put some on a dish, which she set down in front of him.

"Help yourself," she said.

Rollo sipped his tea and ate several of the biscuits.

"This is nice," he said. "Thanks."

"What brings you to Paradise, Mr. Johnson?"

"Summer," he said.

"A vacation?"

"A vacation from Kansas."

"You're from Kansas?"

"Yeah."

"And you'll be doing . . ."

"Mostly, I'll be reading," he said. "Studying the Bible."

"I envy you your reading," Miss Miller said. "Ever since this macular thing got me, my reading has been severely curtailed."

"That's too bad," Rollo said.

Agatha Miller looked closely at him. She found his off-putting appearance and his coarseness unsettling.

"Have you any references, Mr. Johnson? You see, as a woman alone . . ."

"I don't have any, no. I never thought I'd need any," Rollo said. "See, I was planning

76

to stay at a residence hotel. Then I saw your ad. I'll leave now, if you want."

Rollo waited for her answer. There would be consequences if she said he had to leave. He looked inward, listening for the voices, waiting for possible instruction.

Agatha Miller considered the prospect of giving up the only rental opportunity that had, to date, presented itself.

In the end, she overcame her reservations and surrendered to commerce. She needed the money.

"That won't be necessary, Mr. Johnson. I'm sure we can work something out."

Relieved, Rollo said, "That's good."

"Yes," she said.

"Thanks."

"You're very welcome, Mr. Johnson."

"Call me Donnie," Rollo said.

15

Molly left the Civic in roughly the same spot. Peter Perkins sat in his Chevy. Jesse was in his Explorer.

The time passed slowly. Jesse was forced to consider the possibility that the parking-lot murder had caused the crime ring to go to ground.

Then he became aware of the presence of a black BMW sedan. It had already circled the parking lot once and was in the process of doing so again.

Jesse noticed Perkins slide lower in his seat.

In the Explorer, Jesse picked up a news-paper and held it as though he was reading.

The BMW circled the lot for a third time, then slowly descended on the Civic. It pulled to a stop. After several moments, the passenger door opened and a smallish, wiry-looking man got out. The BMW drove away.

The wiry man produced a thin plastic

sleeve, which he inserted between the window and the door frame on the driver's side of the Civic. Within seconds the door was unlocked and the wiry man was inside the car.

He took a pair of screwdrivers from his tool kit. He used them to remove the center console. He leaned over and reached inside with both hands. He fidgeted for several seconds. The Civic roared to life.

The man readjusted himself in the driver's seat. He looked around to make certain no one was watching. Then he pulled out and drove away.

Peter Perkins took up his position as the lead pursuit vehicle. After allowing the Civic a brief head start, he followed.

After several moments, Jesse pulled the Explorer into the traffic flow. He was a dozen car lengths behind Perkins, who was perhaps six or seven lengths behind the Civic.

The Civic drove east on Paradise Boulevard. At Beach Road, it turned left, heading away from town. Merging with other traffic, Perkins lagged far enough behind so as not to alert the driver to the fact he was being followed.

Jesse lagged even farther behind. He called Perkins.

"That you, Jesse?"

"Yes. Make the turnoff as we planned. Did you call in the BMW?"

"I did."

"That's good police work, Pete."

"Thanks, Jesse. Go get 'em."

About a mile up the road, Perkins turned left and abandoned the pursuit. Jesse continued to follow the BMW.

When it reached Paradise Highway, the Civic transitioned onto it, heading north. Jesse slowed and made the same transition.

Fewer cars were now on the road. Instinctively, Jesse dropped farther back so as to barely appear in the Civic's rearview mirror.

They drove like this for twenty or so miles. Then the Civic turned onto Orchard Road with Jesse a safe distance behind.

Orchard was a rural two-lane highway. It ran through a heavily wooded area that was home to a number of farms that were set far back from the road.

Jesse lost sight of the Civic. He slowed and paid particular attention to each driveway he passed. He spotted the tail end of the Civic only moments before it disappeared around the bend of a rutted pathway. He kept going.

He pulled the Explorer to the side of the

road about three-tenths of a mile farther on. There was no other traffic. He turned off the engine and called Perkins.

"Track me, Pete," Jesse said. "The device is activated. When you find the Explorer, park behind it. Alert the troops, as we discussed. If I don't turn up before winter, come find me."

Jesse got out of the Explorer. He strapped on his service belt and proceeded on foot toward the pathway.

16

Jesse stayed close to the shrubbery growing on both sides of the rutted driveway. He moved cautiously, stopping frequently to listen. From a distance he could discern the high-pitched whine of heavy equipment.

He had traveled about a hundred yards when the driveway widened into an open field. Jesse inched closer to the brush and edged his way along the perimeter of the field.

Ten yards ahead, he spotted an unpainted barnlike structure with a corrugated metal roof and heavy-duty double doors at each end. The BMW was parked in front.

Inside the structure stood a hydraulic lift, the kind usually found in a mechanic's garage. The Civic sat atop the lift. Fluid was being funneled from the car into a giant drum. The seats lay on the ground, having been separated from the body of the car.

From his concealed vantage point Jesse

could see that there was no one in the barn. The only sound was that of the fluids as they flowed from the Civic. He worked his way closer.

From a door located on the far wall of the barn, the wiry man suddenly emerged and headed for the lift. He checked the progress of the fluid drip, then turned his attention to the seats. He covered his eyes with goggles and switched on an electric saw. He began to remove the seats from their frame.

Jesse watched for several minutes. The noise of the saw was deafening. He decided to use it as cover.

He removed the truncheon from his service belt. When he was certain that he wasn't in the wiry man's line of sight, he crawled from the bushes and sprinted toward him.

In a sudden explosion of force, Jesse hammered the truncheon into the back of the wiry man's head. He dropped the saw and pitched forward.

Jesse carefully kicked the saw away. He returned the truncheon to his belt. He grabbed the fallen man and dragged him outside.

He gathered the man's arms behind him and wrapped them together with a length of plastic wire. He did the same with the man's legs. He pulled a red-and-white kerchief from his pocket, crushed it into a ball, and stuffed it into the man's mouth. After making certain the man could breathe, Jesse pulled him into the bushes.

Jesse returned to the door and stood behind it, hidden, truncheon in hand. He waited. The deafening noise from the saw continued unabated. It finally caught the attention of the man inside.

The door opened, and the BMW driver stepped through. He noticed the saw on the ground. As he started toward it, Jesse stepped from behind the door and smashed the truncheon into the driver's neck. He fell, facedown.

Jesse walked to the electric saw and yanked its plug from the wall socket. He was hoping that at some point his hearing would return.

He took his cell phone from his pocket, opened it, and hit the speed dial. Peter Perkins answered on the first ring.

"We're a go," Jesse said.

He knelt down beside the driver and checked his condition. Satisfied, he removed the handcuffs from his service belt and used them to clamp the man's wrists together behind him.

He took a blindfold from his pocket and

tied it over the man's eyes.

He searched the driver's pockets and found his wallet.

It identified him as Robert Lopresti, with an address in Fall River, Massachusetts.

A car approached, wheels crunching the driveway. Perkins and Suitcase pulled up in front of the barn. They got out of the Chevy and looked around.

"Chop shop, huh, Jesse," Suitcase said.

"Looks like it," Jesse said.

"Well hidden," Perkins said.

"This one's name is Robert Lopresti," Jesse said. "He's ready to go. You take the BMW, Suit. Keys are in it. I'll look after the other one. Pete, you notify the crew that it's okay to break this place down. See if they can restore the Honda. Let's move."

Perkins and Suitcase picked up Lopresti and placed him in the backseat of the Chevy. Perkins used his handcuffs to bind Lopresti's feet together.

Suitcase got into the BMW. He lowered the passenger-side window and called to Jesse.

"There's a child safety seat in the back," he said.

"All the better," Jesse said.

The BMW fell in line behind the Chevy as they both drove off.

Jesse pulled the wiry man from the bushes. The man was still groggy but beginning to awaken. Jesse removed the binding from the man's wrists and ankles. He also removed the gag.

He looked in the man's wallet, and from his driver's license, made note of the name, Santino Valazza. Also from Fall River.

Jesse left the barely conscious Valazza to fend for himself, then headed back down the driveway toward his Explorer.

Jesse returned to the station and slipped into his office. He looked up as Molly entered carrying a cup of hot coffee, which she placed on his desk.

"Non-precedential," she said, as she sat down. "You look like shit, Jesse."

"It's amazing how much police work agrees with me."

"You're not too old to consider a career change."

"Was there something you wanted, Molly, or did you plant yourself here solely for the entertainment value?"

"I wanted to see how it went."

"So far, so good," Jesse said.

"So we stick with plan A?"

"We do."

"You sure about this, Jesse?"

"Not entirely," he said. "But it's better

than the alternative."

"Which is?"

"Play by the rules and do nothing."

"Well, when you put it that way," she said.

The phone rang, and Molly answered it. She handed it to Jesse.

"Captain Healy," she said, and left the office.

Jesse picked up the call.

"It's on," he said.

17

The safe house was located in a failing neighborhood on the outskirts of town. A bank foreclosure, it had been unoccupied for months. In anticipation of his need, Jesse had earlier arranged to borrow it with the help of his friend Marcy Campbell, a local real-estate broker, who had an in at the bank.

A fair amount of preplanning had gone into the alteration of the house. Jesse had worked with Suitcase and Perkins on it, keeping knowledge of its existence to a small need-to-know list. The three police officers had discussed the questionable legality of what it was they were about to undertake. He had offered both Perkins and Suitcase the chance to back out, which they both declined.

The changes that they made to the house were minimal. They had focused their attention on one small bedroom, the one with an adjoining bath.

They cleaned the room thoroughly. They placed bars on the outside of the room's single window. They removed the door and replaced it with one of their own, which had been fitted with a pair of heavy-duty dead bolts. In the bottom half they fashioned a slot large enough so that food trays could be passed through it. In the top half they installed a one-way mirror.

They removed the shower rod and curtain from the tub. They also removed the towel racks. They stripped the room of anything that might be used as a weapon.

The furniture in the room consisted of a futon, which doubled as both sofa and mattress. A blanket, a towel, and a bathrobe had been placed atop it. There was also a single straight-back chair.

They used a generator to power both the bedroom and the room adjacent to it. This they would use as their base.

Perkins and Suitcase arrived at the house within moments of each other. They parked their vehicles in the multicar garage, from which they could achieve direct access inside.

Together they lifted the now semiconscious Robert Lopresti from the Chevy. They got him on his feet and walked him to the bedroom. They took him inside.

They placed him on the futon. First they removed the binding from both his hands and his feet. Then they removed the blind-fold as well as the rest of his clothing.

Satisfied, they took the blindfold and the clothing and left the room. They locked both of the dead bolts behind them.

18

The tinkling of the piano keys in the Gray Gull was nearly as soft as the lighting.

Jesse stared admiringly at Alexis Richardson. She was wearing a close-fitting black dress that emphasized everything. She was drinking an apple martini. He was having a scotch.

"So then what happened," Jesse said.

"I told him that I wouldn't sleep with him. I said I had earned the grade and that if he refused to give it to me, I would make sure that the dean of students was made aware of certain, shall we say, indiscretions."

"And?"

"I received the grade, and the shithead never bothered me again."

Jesse laughed.

"So you've left a trail of broken hearts."

"Broken desires, perhaps. Not broken hearts."

"Never get too close."

"Something like that," she said.

"Not breaking the hearts of others might ensure that others won't break yours."

"That's too deep for me, Jesse."

"I rest my case," he said.

The waitress brought their dinners. She had the pistachio-crusted salmon; he had steak. They ate slowly.

"What was it you said? You don't speak to your ex-wife," Alexis said.

"Not for a while."

"Because?"

"Because I found myself enabling her to say things which were hurtful."

"Part of her pattern?"

"Exactly. For the longest time I didn't recognize it. I thought we were talking about reconciliation. It was what I was hoping for. Somehow I thought it was what she was hoping for, too. I was wrong."

"And your shrink helped you to see you were wrong?"

"When I took the time to actually listen to him."

Alexis didn't say anything.

"I can at least recognize when I'm not acting in my own best interests," Jesse said. "Dix once told me I was involved in a conspiracy against myself. It made sense."

"Feels good to stop hitting yourself in the head."

"Something like that," he said.

"Are you ever uncertain, Jesse?"

Jesse thought about that.

"Professionally, no. Personally, nearly always," he said.

"Because?"

"Things don't have a tendency to work out well. What about you?"

"The opposite. I don't feel uncertain personally, because I know that a real life would conflict with my career."

"So?"

"So I don't have a real life."

"And professionally?"

"Professionally, I'm a mess."

"Because?"

"The world has changed. Your options in this economy are limited. The stakes are incredibly high. Insecurity dogs you. Fear of failure haunts you. Welcome to the me generation."

Jesse didn't say anything.

"Kickboxing helps reduce the tension. Also fills my violence quota."

"Your violence quota?"

"I imagine each lethal blow as an act of violence against authority."

"What about a tenderness quota?"

"I don't suppose I have one."

"Violence without tenderness doesn't make for a good life balance."

"What about you? Are you tender, Jesse?"

"I was, once."

"And now?"

"I wouldn't know."

19

Rollo walked at night. Late. He left the house by way of the back door, never before midnight.

He walked everywhere and looked at everything. He learned the town. He came to know Paradise as if he had been born there. No one ever saw him. He was invisible.

He made it a point to study every neighborhood. Every commercial center, park, and harbor.

He was as familiar with the yacht club as he was with the Midnight Mission. He took note of every school. He especially studied the police station.

The dark voices were always with Rollo. They controlled him.

When an unattended dog left outside challenged him, it was the voices that commanded him. *Speak kindly to it,* they said. *Make friends with it. Kill it.*

The voices instructed him to initiate a series of events that, by design, would serve to unsettle Paradise.

They informed him that deadly night crimes would frighten people, and by so doing, capture the attention of the Paradise Police Department. And its chief.

On Rollo's behalf, the darkness was conjuring a fury that would soon be unleashed upon Jesse Stone.

20

In the morning, Jesse went directly to the safe house. He parked his Explorer in the garage and headed inside.

Perkins and Suitcase were in the second bedroom. It had been outfitted with a pair of army cots, two chairs, and a table. They would be there for as long as it took.

"Post time," Jesse said.

Through the one-way mirror, he could see Lopresti seated on the futon, wearing the bathrobe.

Perkins called for Lopresti to stand against the far wall with his hands in the air. He unlocked the dead bolts and opened the door. Jesse entered. Perkins closed and re-locked the door behind him.

"Good morning," Jesse said. "You're welcome to stand down from the wall and sit if you like."

Lopresti lowered his hands. He continued to stand. He looked at Jesse.

"I know who you are," he said.

Jesse didn't say anything.

"Why am I here?"

"You're being held," Jesse said.

"I realize that. Why?"

"You have something I want."

"Which is?"

"Information."

"What information?"

"The identity and whereabouts of your employer."

"And if I don't provide that information?"

"Then you'll continue to be held," Jesse said.

"And if I do provide the information?"

"Once it's verified, you'll be released."

"So I'm a hostage."

"I'd rather think of you as a prisoner of war."

"A prisoner of war?"

"Mob war. You know, the good guys versus the bad guys. In case you didn't realize it, you're one of the bad guys. Captured while engaging in an act of war."

"And you're prepared to hold me indefinitely?"

"No."

"What's that supposed to mean?"

"There might come a time when I determine that holding you is fruitless. I sincerely hope that time never comes."

Lopresti didn't say anything.

"How this goes down depends entirely on you, Mr. Lopresti. If you don't wish to share the information with me now, I'll leave. But it's important for you to understand that there's a clock ticking on this circumstance, and I'm not a patient man."

Lopresti remained silent.

"Do you have family?"

Lopresti nodded.

"Kids?"

Again, Lopresti nodded.

"It would be awful for them if they never heard from you again. Or learned of your fate. I sympathize with them. But allow me to make this absolutely clear to you. If you continue to defy me, the consequences will be lethal."

Jesse stood and walked to the door, which Perkins opened. He stepped out of the room, and the door closed behind him. The only sound was that of the dead bolts being relocked.

"What's next," Perkins said.

"We'll give him a little time to cogitate."

"Cogitate," Suitcase said.

"You could look it up," Jesse said.

He left the safe house and drove away.

21

Molly stuck her head into Jesse's office, saw him at his desk, then walked in and sat down.

"You've had phone calls from Captain Healy and Lucy Jameson."

"Who's Lucy Jameson?"

"You don't know?"

"Would I be asking if I did?"

"There goes my five bucks."

"Excuse me?"

"I bet Suitcase she was your current squeeze."

Jesse stared at her.

"Taking recent history into consideration, it wasn't a bad bet," Molly said. "She said she'd call again."

"Did she say what it was about?"

"No. She seemed upset. We thought it was because you'd dumped her."

"Was there anything else?"

"No."

"Good."

Molly stood, sighed, and strolled out of Jesse's office.

Jesse called Healy.

"Do you have anything on a pair of low-lifes from Fall River named Santino Valazza and Robert Lopresti," he said.

"And good morning to you, too."

"Robert Lopresti and Santino Valazza."

"Santino as in Sonny Corleone?"

"Nice existential leap."

"I'm trying to live down the dolt sobriquet."

"Sobriquet?"

"Guy can't try too hard."

"Valazza and Lopresti."

"Does this have something to do with what I think it has to do with?"

"Elliptical, aren't we."

"Might take me a while. I'm the state homicide commander, and I do have work of my own."

"You do?"

"Some. But I've put your name at the top of my to-do list."

"Gee, I had no idea the homicide commander kept such a list."

"He doesn't. I lied. I'll get back to you."

Jesse hung up and sat back in his chair.

"It's Lucy Jameson," Molly said. "Line two."

Jesse answered the call.

"Jesse Stone," he said.

"Chief Stone. Lucy Jameson. I wanted you to know that some son of a bitch killed my Rufus. Snapped his neck like it was a pretzel."

"And Rufus would be . . ."

"My dog."

"Oh," Jesse said. "When did this happen, Ms. Jameson?"

"Lucy."

"When did this happen, Lucy?"

"Last night. I found him this morning."

"Have you any idea who might have done it? A neighbor? An enemy? Anyone?"

"Rufus did his share of barking, I will say that. But folks around here weren't upset by him. He wasn't vicious. He wasn't a biter. I can't imagine who could have done such a thing."

"I'm terribly sorry for your loss, Ms. Jameson. Lucy. I'll send one of my officers. Perhaps he might be of service."

"Thank you."

Jesse called for Rich Bauer, who quickly appeared in his doorway.

"Go take a look at Lucy Jameson's dog,

will you, Rich? Maybe you can detect something."

"You bet, Skipper," Bauer said.

"Rich," Jesse said, "may I ask you a favor?"

"A favor? Sure thing, Skipper. Name it."

"Quit calling me Skipper."

Jesse left the office and drove off in his cruiser. He needed some down time, and he chose to take it patrolling Paradise in search of miscreants. Showing the flag, so to speak.

He found a few illegally parked cars and stopped to write the citations. He took comfort in the unseemly chore of writing parking tickets.

He thought about the Robert Lopresti adventure. He knew he was operating outside of the law. Ironically, as a small-town police chief, Jesse had always believed that acting outside of the law was a perk. He was well aware of the personal risk he was taking. But he was intent on stirring the pot.

Gino Fish ran organized crime in Massachusetts. Gambling, prostitution, vending machines, construction, sanitation. He had relinquished narcotics because they were against his principles.

Although he didn't know who was running the car theft operation, Jesse was certain that Gino Fish was pulling the strings from behind the scenes. Perhaps a meeting with him was in order.

He wrote another handful of tickets, then went home.

It was after dark when Molly Crane finished work and was finally able to leave the station. Everyone else had already gone.

She went around the office turning off lights. She checked to make certain the coffeemaker was off. She grabbed her coat and her bag and left the building.

Once outside, she locked the door behind her. She took a couple of deep breaths and headed for her car.

Then she stopped and stood still. She looked around. She thought she heard something. She listened for a few moments. Then she walked to her car. After looking around once again, she got in and drove away.

Secure in the knowledge that she was gone, Rollo Nurse slipped out of the hedges alongside the building.

Not yet, the voices had said to him.

22

Once home, Jesse put away his paraphernalia, and began to straighten up the house. He wore a T-shirt and boxer shorts, and was feeding the cat when he heard knocking on his door.

"Dammit," he said.

He picked up his pistol from the kitchen console and press-checked it on his way to the door.

He was stopped dead in his tracks by the appearance of Alexis Richardson. She stood in the doorway, a sack of Chinese takeout in her hand.

"Nice outfit," she said.

Jesse looked at her.

"I took a chance," she said.

He didn't say anything.

"I always find Chinese a safe bet. You haven't eaten, have you?"

Jesse stared at her.

"Are you going to ask me in or shoot me,"

she said.

Jesse realized that his pistol was still in his hand.

He lowered it. Then he opened the door wider so she could enter.

She stepped inside.

He looked down at himself for a moment. Then he looked up at her.

"I'll be right back," he said.

When Jesse went upstairs, Alexis wandered into the living room.

"I've never actually been inside the home of a police chief before," she called to him.

When he didn't respond, she stopped to look at the picture of Ozzie Smith which hung on the wall above the fireplace. She studied it for a while. It was an incredible photo. It created the illusion that the Hall of Famer was flying. His body was floating lengthwise in the air, hovering above the ground, his glove hand extended, a caught ball lodged inside the glove.

When Jesse returned, wearing khakis and a blue shirt that he hadn't tucked in, she asked him about it.

"He was the best shortstop I ever saw," Jesse said.

"And you wanted to be like him," she said.

"I was never that good," he said. "All I wanted was to make the show. Have a shot."

"But you got hurt," she said.

"My shoulder," he said.

"Do you miss it?"

"Every day."

They wandered over to the French doors.

"It's very secluded here," Alexis said.

"I like secluded," Jesse said.

"Am I safe in the assumption that you live here alone?"

"Of late, there's been a cat hovering about. Other than that, you're safe."

He suddenly remembered his manners.

"Forgive me," he said. "Can I get you anything?"

"You can take the food," she said.

He took the food.

"Is there vodka," she said.

"I think so."

"You think so? You mean you don't know for certain?"

"I'm a big-picture guy," he said. "Sometimes the small stuff eludes me."

"I guess that eliminates the possibility of tonic."

"Not necessarily. Let me go look."

He left her and went to the kitchen.

When he returned, he found her outside on the porch.

He was carrying a vodka and tonic, garnished by a slice of a somewhat tired lime.

He stepped outside.

He was surprised to see her holding the black-and-white cat. She was seated on the love seat, and the cat was nestled comfortably on her lap, where it allowed itself to be petted. It appeared to be purring.

"I love cats," she said.

Jesse didn't say anything.

He started toward the love seat, but somehow the cat misunderstood and, without warning, it leapt from Alexis's lap and jumped off the porch.

"We just recently met," Jesse said. "It likes what I feed it, but it's very standoffish."

"Be patient," Alexis said.

She stood up and walked over to him. She took the drink from his hand and sipped it. Then she put it down.

She placed her arms around his neck and kissed him.

She leaned back and looked in his eyes.

"Hello, Jesse Stone," she said.

Then she kissed him again.

He kissed her back. She tasted of vodka and tonic and old lime and life.

"I hardly know you," he said.

She looked at him.

"Who are you, Alexis?"

"I'm an ambitious careerist who finds herself in a strange town and has discovered a mysterious man whom she finds attractive."

"I don't think it's such a good idea."

She looked at him.

"Why," she said.

"I'm unreliable," he said.

"Me, too," she said.

"I'll run at the first sign of trouble," he said.

"Me, too," she said.

"Aw, hell," he said.

He kissed her. Then he kissed her again.

"Be tender, Jesse," she said.

He looked at her for a moment.

Then he picked her up and carried her upstairs.

Afterward they feasted on Chinese. Jesse wore his boxer shorts; Alexis wore his T-shirt. They ate prodigious amounts of kung pao shrimp, chicken in garlic sauce, and barbecued beef, which they washed down with several bottles of Tsingtao beer, which Jesse kept on ice.

"How is it you're not spoken for, post-Jenn," Alexis said.

"I thought I was. But I don't think so anymore."

"Who?"

"A private detective from Boston. I met

her on a case. She's somewhere in Europe now. Have you heard of the movie actress Moira Harris?"

Alexis shrugged.

"Moira Harris was shooting a picture in Boston, and Sunny was hired as her security."

"Sunny?"

"Sunny Randall," Jesse said. "Moira got a movie shooting in London and Prague. She asked for Sunny. That's where she is now."

"Do you love her?"

"That's a loaded question. There was a time when I thought we'd be together. She thought so, too. But somehow things didn't go that way."

"Why?"

"History, I guess. Each of our marriages had ended badly. We were both damaged goods. All the king's horses and all the king's men . . . We couldn't be put back together again. We tried. Then she took the movie. When she left, I thought I'd miss her, but I don't, really. Out of sight, out of mind, I suppose."

"Are you over her?"

"I don't know," Jesse said.

Alexis didn't say anything.

"And you? Have you ever been married," Jesse said.

"God, no. Married to a job, perhaps. I'm not a good catch. I'm an anathema. Guys take one look at me and start clutching their balls."

They sat silently for a while.

"Thank you for being honest," she said.

Jesse didn't say anything.

Alexis stood up and walked over to his chair. She insinuated herself onto his lap.

"That kind of honesty is rare in a man."

Jesse didn't say anything.

She leaned back and looked at him. She traced his cheek with her finger. She kissed him.

After a while they went back upstairs.

23

When Jesse arrived at his office, Molly was already on her feet.

"Coffee," Jesse said.

"Dogs," Molly said.

"Excuse me?"

"Two of 'em. Necks broken. Different parts of town. Owners phoned this morning."

"Coffee," Jesse said.

"I'll walk with you," Molly said.

With Molly at his side, Jesse headed for the coffeemaker. As he poured himself a cup, he noticed a box of donuts sitting on the sideboard. He grabbed one.

She watched him. He took a bite.

"Yum," he said.

She stared at him, disapprovingly.

"Those'll kill you," she said.

"Yeah," he said. "But what a way to go."

"Death by lard," she said. "How pleasant for you."

He looked at her. Then he went back to his office. She followed.

"I've been meaning to ask you something," Jesse said.

"What," Molly said.

"We do have intercom capability on our phone system, don't we," he said.

She looked at him.

"Why have we stopped using it," he said.

"Why have we stopped using the intercom?"

"Yes."

Molly didn't say anything.

"You answer most of the calls that come in to the station, correct?"

"Yes."

"You always ask who's calling, right?"

"Where is this leading, Jesse?"

"Every time there's an incoming call, you answer it and then you shout out the name of who's calling. And who it's for. Do you think it's possible that shouting might not be the most effective way of alerting our personnel to incoming calls?"

"Do I need an Internal Affairs representative present for this conversation?"

"Would you ever consider placing an incoming call on hold and then notifying the recipient by use of the intercom?"

"Would I get paid more?"

"Do you think it's possible we could attempt an experiment involving the intercom?"

"Are you instructing me to use it," Molly said.

"I wouldn't put it that way."

"What way would you put it?"

"I'd like you to try using the intercom."

"I don't like the intercom."

Jesse didn't say anything.

"Are you instructing me to use the intercom," Molly said.

"No. I'm asking."

"You're not instructing."

"No."

"I'll take it under advisement," she said, and stood up.

As she was leaving, she looked back over her shoulder and shouted, "Rich Bauer phoned."

Jesse stared at her.

Then he returned Bauer's call.

"The dogs, Jesse," he said. "It's awful."

"How awful?"

"Awful. Whoever killed them really meant to do it."

"Similarities?"

"Broken necks. How could anyone do that to a dog?"

"Takes all kinds, Rich."

"What are we gonna do?"

"We're gonna find who did it is what we're gonna do," Jesse said.

24

"You're here because you're feeling overwhelmed," Dix said.

"I didn't say that."

"What did you say?"

"I said things had heated up somewhat."

"So you don't feel overwhelmed?"

"I didn't say that."

"Why does this have to be so hard," Dix said.

"I'm feeling stressed," Jesse said.

"How are you handling the stress?"

"I'm talking to you."

"You may be talking, but you're not saying anything," Dix said.

Jesse didn't say anything.

"This car business. How are you handling it?"

"Unconventionally."

Dix didn't say anything.

"I don't want to talk about it," Jesse said.

"Tell me again why you came here."

"To talk."

"Perhaps I'm missing something."

"Let's put it this way. Let's say that I'm baiting a trap."

"Will this trap place you in harm's way?"

"It might."

"So you feel vulnerable," Dix said.

"I didn't say that."

"How do you feel about it?"

"How do I feel?"

Dix didn't say anything.

"Anxious," Jesse said.

"You feel anxious?"

"Yes."

"How do you handle it?"

"The anxiety?"

"Yes."

"I handle it," Jesse said.

"But you're experiencing a great deal of it," Dix said.

"Only on occasion."

After a pause, Dix said, "Are you drinking?"

"Not really."

"Are you sticking to your rule?"

"What rule?"

"The two-drinks-a-night rule. This is brutal."

"Mostly I'm only having one a night."

"So you're not drinking?"

"I overstepped my limit the one time."

"After the parking-lot killing," Dix said.

"I couldn't get the image of the widow out of my mind. She was so grief-stricken. She was trying to hold it together, but the worst was yet to come, and I could see in her eyes that she knew it."

"So you got drunk?"

"Yes."

"But you haven't gotten drunk again?"

"No."

Dix didn't say anything.

"I identified with her grief."

"Jenn?"

"Yes."

Neither of them said anything.

"I regretted it," Jesse said. "I'm determined not to let her get to me again."

They sat silently for a while.

"Is there anything else you want to tell me," Dix said.

"I've started seeing someone."

"Someone other than Sunny Randall?"

"Yes."

"So you're not seeing Sunny any longer?"

"She's away."

"If she were here?"

"I don't know."

"Why?"

"I flew too close to the flame."

"Which means?"

"I like it better where it's cooler."

Dix didn't say anything.

"I don't think I'm ready."

They sat quietly for a while.

"Do you take these sessions seriously," Dix said.

"I do," Jesse said.

"Do you find them helpful?"

"Mostly."

"Do you reflect on them?"

"Sometimes. Why?"

"Because you're often obtuse."

Jesse didn't say anything.

"I don't want you to wander off the path toward self-realization," Dix said.

"It's when I wander that I come to see you."

"Which is a good thing."

"If you say so."

25

Jesse returned to the safe house. He parked in the garage and went inside.

Everything was as it had been except that both Perkins and Suit now had two days' worth of beard.

"Anything I should know about," Jesse said.

"He's agitated. He's been asking for you," Suitcase said.

"That's a start," Jesse said.

They went to the door and watched Lopresti for a while.

He, too, needed a shave. Jesse went into the room.

"Good morning," he said.

"Where were you? Why in hell did you take so long to come back?"

"Did you miss me?"

"Don't fuck with me."

"Do you have something to tell me?"

"I might."

"I'll want to know several things, but first I'd like to learn who you're working for."

"How do I know that you'll let me go if I tell you," Lopresti said.

"You don't."

"You said something about verifying what I might tell you. How does that happen?"

"That's my concern."

"How much information will I have to give you?"

"Enough to satisfy me."

"You don't give an inch, do you?"

"Someone has died because of this business, Robert. I intend to put a stop to it. If you help me, you'll go free. You'll have to trust in that."

Lopresti thought about it. "John Lombardo," he said.

"How do I find John Lombardo?"

"I don't know. He finds me."

"That's not good enough, Robert."

"Listen, I don't know how to find him. If I need him, I call his cell."

"What's the number?"

Jesse wrote it down as Lopresti recited it.

"How did you come to know Mr. Lombardo," Jesse said.

"Fall River. I was workin' the streets. Me and Santino. Every now and then we'd lift a car. Mostly just to see if we could. I knew a guy was interested in parts. We'd sell the cars to him."

"And?"

"And this one time we brought in a car and our friend told us that Mr. Lombardo might have work for us."

Jesse didn't say anything.

"So we met with him. He asked if we'd like to join his operation. The money was good. So we did," Lopresti said.

"How long ago was that?"

"Six months or so."

"And you've been working for him ever since?"

"Yeah."

"Where?"

"What?"

"Where have you been working," Jesse said.

"Here and there. No one place."

"Until you set up shop in Paradise."

"Yeah."

"Which you did because . . . ?"

"Because Mr. Lombardo said to. He said he wanted to find a new place for a shop. He mentioned Paradise. He purchased the farm and told us to work there."

"Where do I find Mr. Lombardo?"

"I already told you I don't know."

"Did you ever meet him in Boston," Jesse said.

"Yeah."

"Where?"

"At a restaurant."

"What restaurant?"

"Some place he likes in Cambridge."

"What place?"

"An Italian place. Il Capriccio. On Ash Street. Go verify this shit, will ya? My wife must be climbin' the walls."

"Who killed Mike Lytell," Jesse said.

"Who the fuck is Mike Lytell?"

"Guy killed in the carjack."

"How would I know?"

"Because you do."

Lopresti didn't say anything.

"The name of Lytell's killer," Jesse said.

When Lopresti remained silent, Jesse stood up to leave. He walked to the door.

"Petey Marcovy," Lopresti said.

"Russian?"

"Yeah."

"Peter Marcovy?"

"Pyotr. P-Y-O-T-R. Everyone called him Petey," Lopresti said.

"Also from Fall River?"

"By way of the Ukraine. You won't find him, though."

"What?"

"You're not gonna find him. He's dead."

Jesse didn't say anything.

"Mr. Lombardo had him shot. Petey was a new guy. A hothead. Mr. Lombardo had enough of him."

"More likely he didn't want Petey identifying him," Jesse said. "Sharks feeding on their young."

"Yeah, well, I'm hoping that because of you they don't start feeding on me."

"Life's a bitch, ain't it?"

26

Jesse phoned Healy from the car.

"Bingo," he said.

"Gee, and all I needed was N-thirty-five."

"You ever hear of a connected guy called John Lombardo?"

"Not offhand."

"Our POW gave him up. Fall River guy."

"I'll check it out. Don't do anything foolish, Jesse," Healy said. "Let me at least get the skinny on him."

"You know where to find me," Jesse said, and ended the call.

Jesse pulled up in front of the Town Hall and parked in the no-parking zone. He found Carter Hansen in his office, eating a brown-bagged lunch.

"May I interrupt your lunch," Jesse said.

"If I said no?"

"I'd come in anyway."

"Why don't you come in, then," Hansen said.

"I'd like to borrow the services of Alexis Richardson."

"Excuse me?"

"You mentioned that she was adroit in the field of public relations."

"I can't remember ever using the word *adroit.*"

"Forgive me. I must have you confused with someone else. Well?"

"Well what?"

"Is she adroit in the field of public relations?"

"That would depend upon your definition of adroit."

"This isn't going well."

"What is it you want, Stone?"

"I want Ms. Richardson to prepare a press release."

"What kind of press release?"

"One advising the population of Paradise to keep their dogs inside at night."

Hansen didn't say anything.

"Well?"

After a moment Hansen picked up the phone and dialed a number.

"Marilyn," he said. "Would you ask Alexis if she could step into my office for a moment?"

The two men sat in silence. Then Alexis Richardson walked in. Jesse stood.

"You remember Chief Stone, don't you," Hansen said.

"I might," she said. "Chief Stone."

"Jesse."

"Jesse. It's nice to see you again," she said.

"It's nice to see you again," Jesse said.

"All right," Hansen said. "We can dispense with the hooyah. Chief Stone wants you to prepare a press release for him."

"Regarding?"

"I'd like to catch the attention of the dog-owning population of Paradise. I want to advise them to keep their dogs inside after dark."

"Is this related to the recent dog killings," Alexis said.

"You know about the dog killings?"

"Small town. I'd be happy to help you, Jesse. If it's all right with you, Unc— uh, Selectman Hansen, perhaps Chief Stone could join me in my office."

"Fine. That would be fine. Good day, Chief Stone."

Alexis and Jesse left Hansen's office. Once they were outside, Jesse murmured under his breath, "Good day to you, too, Uncle Carter."

Alexis punched him on the arm.

■ ■ ■ ■

Once in her office, Jesse closed the door. He took her in his arms and kissed her. She returned the kiss.

"I suppose doing it on your desk would be out of the question," Jesse said.

"Only during business hours," she said.

"About the press release," Jesse said.

He told her how to word it. He wanted to alert the newspapers, TV and radio stations, and the alternative media. He wanted flyers printed and posted in the library, the supermarkets, the coffee shops, and especially in the pet stores and veterinarians' offices. He didn't want to frighten people, just make them aware of a potential danger.

She promised to attend to it immediately. She hoped to make the evening news and appear in all of the next day's papers.

"That kiss was intriguing," she said. "I was wondering if we might continue it this evening."

"I'd have to check my schedule," he said.

She put her arms around his neck and kissed him.

"Should I bring Chinese?"

"There's an idea," Jesse said.

27

In the morning, after Alexis had left, Jesse went about his chores, which included feeding the cat. By now an uneasy truce had developed between them. The cat would sit on the love seat, watching as Jesse put out the food. It appeared ready to leap at the slightest provocation. Jesse would pretend to ignore it.

But on this morning, as Jesse was setting out a bowl of wet cat food, the cat jumped from the love seat and began rubbing itself against Jesse's legs, its tail standing straight up, shimmying.

Jesse reached down and ran his hand over the cat's back. It rubbed itself against him even harder. This went on for several moments, until the cat emitted a throaty croak. It then approached the dish and crouched down to eat.

Jesse smiled.

By the time he reached the office, there had been three calls regarding strangled dogs.

He was sitting in his office, surrounded by Molly Crane, Rich Bauer, Steve Lesnick, and Arthur Angstrom. Everyone but Molly was eating a donut.

"I want to establish a night patrol," Jesse said. "I want two units on duty from ten p.m. to six a.m. Unmarked vehicles. Divide the town in half. One half per unit. Circle each half constantly, randomly, always on the lookout for something that appears strange."

"Who's gonna man these patrols," Molly said.

"Rich will be in charge. He'll take the lead vehicle. I want summer hires in the second."

"What are we supposed to do if we do notice anything strange," Bauer said.

"Bust it," Jesse said.

"You mean make an arrest, Skipper," Bauer said. "Uh, Jesse," he quickly added.

"Correct."

"What if we're wrong?"

"Better to be safe than sorry," Jesse said. "If a mistake is made, so be it."

"When do you want this to start," Molly said.

"Tonight."

The phone rang, and Molly went to her desk to answer it.

She called out to Jesse.

"Captain Healy on two," she said.

Jesse looked at her.

"What happened to 'I'll try it,' " Jesse said.

"Try what," Molly said.

"The intercom."

"I forgot."

"You didn't forget," Jesse said.

"Are you suggesting that I purposely refused to use the intercom?"

"I am."

"Some nerve," she said.

The others filed out of his office as Jesse picked up the call.

"Jesse," he said.

"John Lombardo," Healy said. "Interesting fellow. Definitely on the come. He appears to be connected to Gino Fish. My OC guys tell me he did a number of small jobs for Gino and has since graduated to more important stuff."

"Such as?"

"He was linked to the construction rackets in the southern part of the state. In the Fall River area. We have reason to believe he may have done some wet work there. He seems to have recently moved to the Boston area. He drew attention making collections involving a few high rollers who had reneged on their obligations."

"Which entailed?"

"In one instance, it entailed death. Which appeared enough to frighten the other recalcitrants into paying up," Healy said.

"Is there anything to link him to automobile theft?"

"Not here. At least not yet. But he does have a track record in Fall River, which could indicate that he might be a person of interest."

"Any idea where he can be found?"

"We're still working on that."

"You'll let me know when you have something?"

"Top of my list."

"That's hopeful."

"This guy is the real deal, Jesse. He's lethal, and he's not afraid to let people know it. He's making a name for himself."

"Mr. Lombardo may be misguided if he thinks he can put that name up in lights here in Paradise," Jesse said.

"He probably doesn't know that."

"He will."

28

Rollo sensed the change. First there were the stories in the newspapers. On the TV. Then the flyers in the stores. He knew it was time.

That night, carrying a small bag that he had earlier prepared, Rollo headed for Paradise Harbor. He melted into the shadows whenever he saw headlights. He had already noticed that the streets were now being patrolled. He took extra precautions to conceal himself.

Once at the harbor, Rollo made his way to one of the boardwalk refreshment stands. Each of them offered a different kind of fare. One had tacos. One had ice cream and cakes. One had burgers and fries. He had chosen the one that offered the burgers and fries.

Benny's Burgers. A shack, really. Wooden. The front end had a service window, which was boarded up at night.

The back end contained the grills and the fryers and a storage area.

The front end faced the boardwalk. The back opened onto the ocean.

There was no one on the boardwalk at two a.m. Just Rollo, standing behind the burger shack.

A fair amount of detritus had been collected and deposited behind the shack. Large plastic bags filled with garbage were awaiting early-morning pickup. Empty bottles and cans had been collected and stored in recycling bins.

The shack's back door did not close properly. It wasn't flush with the baseboard. Not only was there a gap at the bottom, but the door itself had warped and bowed at the top. It was a suitable target for Rollo.

First he withdrew two rolls of toilet paper from his bag. Then he took out two large cans of lighter fluid. Placing the nozzle of the first can through the gap at the bottom of the door, he sprayed nearly its entire contents inside the shack.

Then he unraveled the first roll of toilet paper and shoved as much of it as he could through the gap and into the shack. He then sprayed the remainder of the fluid on the paper and onto the door itself.

He unraveled the second roll of toilet

paper, placing it in strips at the top of the door and also through a small opening that the bowed door provided. Whatever paper remained he placed on top of and below the garbage bags.

Using the second can of lighter fluid, he sprayed the door and then created a line of fluid trailing from underneath the door to a spot perhaps five feet away from it.

Satisfied, he wiped the two cans with Kleenex, thereby either smudging or removing any fingerprints. He placed the cans on top of the garbage bags.

He then pulled out a fireplace lighter. He tested it. It worked. He knelt down and ignited the line.

The fluid caught, and the fire raced along the line toward the shack. Once it reached the doused toilet paper, it roared into flame.

Rollo stepped back and watched the flames grow in intensity as they were fed by the fluid and the paper. The fire jumped to the garbage bags. The shack became an inferno.

Rollo retired to the shadows and quickly left the area. Once away from the harbor but within sight of it, he turned back to see what he had wrought. Benny's Burgers was ablaze. The fire had burned its way through the rear of the shack and was now furiously heading forward.

When it reached the deep fryers, the fire began to roar with a greater intensity. Then it appeared to die down.

All of a sudden an earsplitting explosion occurred. Fire and debris filled the night sky. Burning embers flew about, some landing on one of the nearby shacks, igniting it.

As Rollo hurried into the darkness, he could see the illumination in the night sky caused by the flaming harbor. The sound of sirens filled the air as the first engines raced toward the scene.

Rollo was certain that the voices had guided him correctly.

Fury. Destruction.

And this was still the beginning.

"It's only a matter of time, Jesse Stone," he said.

29

Jesse had recruited Molly to accompany him. The reservation was for eight o'clock. She arrived conservatively dressed in a nicely tailored suit, carrying a practical handbag and wearing sensible shoes. Jesse wore his blue suit.

They parked half a block away and walked to Il Capriccio. The maître d' showed them to a corner table that offered a view of the room.

When the waiter appeared with the menus, they each ordered a glass of Chianti. Jesse took in the restaurant.

He guessed it was nearly two-thirds full, not bad for a weeknight during tough economic times. A faint hint of music served as the background for the conversation and laughter that filled the room.

The center table was unoccupied, although Jesse noticed a "Reserved" sign on it. It had been set for eight people.

The waiter brought the wine and took Molly's and Jesse's orders. Lasagna for her, veal piccata for him.

"Who sits at the center table," Jesse said. "Ben Affleck?"

The waiter laughed.

"I'm afraid not," he said. "It's always reserved for one of our regulars."

The waiter left.

Jesse looked up in time to see the party of eight being ushered to the center table. All eight diners were men; all were dressed in silk suits and ties. He quickly saw that seven of the men behaved in a deferential manner toward the eighth.

The eighth was a big man. Someone who had obviously started with a weight problem and had done nothing over time to curb it. He must have weighed three hundred pounds, and from the way he was examining the specials board, it was obvious how seriously he regarded his food.

"It's time," Jesse said. "Do you have the number?"

"The one you gave me," Molly said.

"Yes."

"You want me to go into the ladies' room to make the call. And I'm to hang up as soon as the call is answered."

"Roger."

138

"Wilco," she said.

Molly left the table. Jesse leaned back in his chair and took a sip of wine. His eyes were glued to the big man.

Although Jesse hadn't heard a ring, the man suddenly reached into the breast pocket of his jacket and pulled out a cell phone. He opened it and said something into it. After a moment, he looked at the phone and then closed it. He held it for a while, then returned it to his pocket. His attention returned to the menu.

Molly came back and sat down. "Well," she said.

"Molto bene," Jesse said.

"Which means?"

"Bingo."

"Why didn't you say so?"

30

Jesse spent a good portion of the next day at the site of the harbor fire, which had caused a significant amount of damage. In addition to completely destroying two concession stands, it had also burned clear through the boardwalk.

"Arson," Mickey Kurtz, the Paradise fire captain, said. "Middle-of-the-night hit-and-run. Guy was outta here before the fire even caught."

"Pro," Jesse said.

"Uncertain," Kurtz said.

"Prints?"

"Nah. All we found were a couple of charred lighter-fluid cans. Any possible prints had been burned off."

"Insurance fire?"

"It doesn't appear as such," Kurtz said. "Benny was doing a healthy business in a prime location. It wouldn't make sense."

"Vengeance?"

"That would be a policeman question, not a fireman question."

"So what good are you guys," Jesse said.

"Mostly we're good at putting the suckers out. Also sliding down poles," Kurtz said.

"Impressive skill set," Jesse said.

"Saves a lot of wear and tear on the legs."

"Hell on the scrotum, though," Jesse said. "You'll let me know if forensics turns up any other useful information?"

"I'll send you a copy of the report."

"Thanks, Mick," Jesse said.

"At least no one was killed," Kurtz said.

"At least there's that," Jesse said.

That night Jesse was back at Il Capriccio but not as a customer. He had parked within sight of the restaurant in the hope that John Lombardo would return.

Jesse was slouched in the driver's seat of his Explorer, drinking coffee and thinking, when he spotted the arrival of a pair of black Mercedes-Benz sedans. Both sedans pulled up in front of the restaurant. A man and a woman emerged from each. The two cars then disappeared into the night.

Jesse watched intently as the two couples went inside. It was John Lombardo who led the procession.

Once they were inside, Jesse sat back and

thought more about the fire. It gnawed at him. As was the case with the seemingly random killings of the dogs, he was unable to identify a motive. Something seemed hinky, but he couldn't get a handle on it.

He realized that his attention had drifted when he heard laughter coming from Il Capriccio. Standing in front of the restaurant was the John Lombardo party, the women talking quietly, the men laughing raucously. The Mercedes sedans sped up Ash Street and pulled to a stop.

The women embraced, and the men clapped each other on the back. They each got into their respective sedans and rode away.

Jesse waited for a moment, then fell in behind the Lombardo car. He followed as it drove deeper into residential Cambridge. It wasn't long before it turned into an exclusive area that featured multimillion-dollar homes.

The Mercedes stopped in front of a two-story Colonial-style house that appeared to have been recently restored.

Jesse drove by the house and made note of the address. He drove past the corner and onto the next block, where he turned around, shut off his headlights, and drifted back to a spot from which he could see the

Mercedes. He watched as the Lombardos signaled their good nights and went inside the house. The Mercedes pulled away.

Jesse watched until the lights in the house went out. Then he went home himself.

31

By six the next morning, Jesse had resumed his vigil at the Lombardo house. He was armed with a thermos of coffee and a box of donuts.

At exactly eight o'clock, a Mercedes sedan pulled into the driveway of the house. John Lombardo came out and got into the rear seat. The car backed out of the driveway and pulled away. After a beat, Jesse followed.

The Mercedes made its way through Cambridge, crossed the Charles River into Boston, and headed across town to the Old Harbor. After winding its way through a maze of side streets, it pulled to a stop on Rowe's Wharf, in front of a converted warehouse. John Lombardo emerged from the sedan and went inside.

Jesse parked in front of a fire hydrant, got out of the Explorer, and walked to the warehouse. As he passed, he took note of the name on the door: Zenith Enterprises. Which appeared to be the building's sole occupant. He returned to the Explorer and drove away.

He was back at the station by mid-morning. Once in his office, he was greeted by Molly, who wandered in and sat down.

"Which do you want first, the good news or the bad news," she said.

"Is there a difference," Jesse said.

"Not this morning," she said. "Carter Hansen wants to see you."

"What's the good news?"

"I lost four pounds."

"Is there anything else?"

"Another dog."

"And?"

"What are you gonna do about the dogs, Jesse?"

"What does Bauer say?"

"He and Denny Lange drove around all night and didn't see a thing."

"Put Alexis Richardson on the call list," Jesse said.

"The call list?"

"Whatever list you keep the phone calls on."

"I don't keep a list."

"Then how do you know who's called?"

"I have a message pad."

"Well, put Alexis's name on the message pad."

"Would that be business or personal?"

"Must you always find a way to bust my balls," Jesse said.

"Job wouldn't be any fun otherwise."

"Never mind."

"Never mind what?"

"I'll call Alexis myself."

Molly stood.

"I knew it was personal," she said, and left the office.

Jesse sighed.

Then he called Alexis Richardson.

"Where have you been," she said.

"Fighting crime," he said. "But I can't foresee a crime spree this evening."

"Is that good news?"

"It is for those who lust."

"Which would include?"

"Us."

"I'm glad to see you've got your priorities straight. Was that why you phoned?"

"Yes and no."

"What's the no part?"

"I need you to step up your public-relations efforts," said Jesse.

"Meaning?"

"This dog vendetta continues, and I want

to make certain that we do everything we can to tell people to keep their animals indoors after dark."

"You can count on me," Alexis said.

"I do," Jesse said.

"And the yes part?"

"Did I mention lust," he said.

Jesse arrived at the Town Hall and went directly to the meeting room. There he found Carter Hansen, Morris Comden, and Hasty Hathaway. No stenographer was present.

"Would you care to tell us about what's going on," Hansen said, without any preamble.

"About what," Jesse said.

"We appear to be weathering a storm of animal killings."

"We are," Jesse said.

"What are you doing about it?"

"We've begun a regular night patrol. We've launched a major PR campaign asking the public to bring their animals indoors at night."

"What about the fire?"

"What about the fire," Jesse said.

"What are you doing about it," asked Hansen.

"I'm waiting for the complete forensics

report. Perhaps it will contain a clue."

"And the car thefts," Hasty said.

"I'm working on that also," Jesse said.

"None of these answers seem to indicate you're making any real progress," Hansen said.

Jesse didn't say anything.

"We pay you to deliver results, Chief Stone," Hansen said. "We're entering our most important season, and we seem to be plagued by a series of image-damaging events."

Jesse didn't say anything.

"Well, dammit, what are we going to do? We can't afford to frighten the tourists away."

"We're going to continue to investigate these matters," Jesse said.

"And if you can't bring us results?"

"Then you can fire me."

"Wait a minute. Wait a minute," Hasty said. "Nobody said anything about firing you. Mr. Hansen has some serious concerns, as I'm sure you can appreciate."

Jesse said nothing.

"Work with us, Jesse," Hasty said. "Is that too much to ask? We're all a bit nervous here."

"Everything that can be done is being done," Jesse said.

"You'll keep us in the loop," Hasty said.

"When there's a loop to keep you in," Jesse said.

No one said anything.

Jesse stood up.

"If there's nothing else . . ." he said.

Hansen shook his head.

Comden said nothing.

"We appreciate all that you're doing," Hasty said.

32

Once back in the office, Jesse phoned Captain Healy.

"Zenith Enterprises," Jesse said.

"Television manufacturer," Healy said.

"John Lombardo works out of a converted warehouse at the Old Harbor. The name on the door reads Zenith Enterprises."

"Why didn't you say so?"

"Can you push this to the top of your list?"

"You know what I'm thinking," Healy said.

"What are you thinking?"

"I'm thinking of having new business cards printed."

Jesse waited.

"State homicide commander and personal research assistant. How does that sound?"

"Beneath you," Jesse said.

"Should I ask how you found out where Lombardo works," Healy asked.

"Not if you want to claim deniability."

"I'll see what I can learn," he said.

The next call he made was to Suitcase.

"What's up, Jesse," Suitcase said.

"Tomorrow morning. Three-thirty a.m. I'd like you to awaken our friend, pass his clothes through the food slot, and tell him he's got five minutes to get dressed."

"What are you gonna do?"

"I'm gonna keep him stewing for another half hour, then you and I are gonna pull him out and deliver him elsewhere," Jesse said.

"So all this will be over?"

"Yep. You and Pete can pack up, and when we've gone, Pete can close it down."

"Where are we taking him, Jesse?"

"It's a surprise. I want him ready to leave at four. With his blindfold on and his hands cuffed behind his back."

"He'll be ready."

Jesse arrived at four. He parked and went inside. He found Lopresti dressed, cuffed, and blindfolded.

Jesse went into the room.

"Morning," he said.

"Why am I wearing the blindfold?"

Jesse didn't say anything.

"What about my family? You told me that if I did what you said, I'd be released. You're

151

gonna kill me, aren't you," said Lopresti.

"No," Jesse said. "But if I were you, I'd make it my business not to return to Paradise. If I see you here, regardless of the circumstances, that's when I'll kill you."

Jesse and Suitcase walked Lopresti to the Explorer. Suitcase got behind the wheel. Lopresti sat in the passenger seat. Jesse was in back.

They drove to the Boston warehouse, arriving just before dawn. Once there, Jesse pulled Lopresti from the vehicle. He removed the handcuffs.

"Keep the blindfold on for five minutes. If you attempt to remove it before the five minutes are up, you'll be accosted. It's been nice knowing you, Robert."

Jesse got into the Explorer, and Suitcase drove away. When they turned the corner, Jesse noticed through the rearview mirror that Lopresti was still wearing the blindfold.

On their way back to Paradise, Jesse and Suitcase stopped for breakfast at a highway coffee shop.

"Can I ask a question," Suitcase said over eggs and coffee.

"Go," Jesse said.

"Tell me again why we did it?"

"Why we did what?"

"Held Lopresti like that."

"As a preemptive measure."

"Preemptive of what?"

"A certain Boston-based crime organization is in the process of expanding its activities. Under the guidance of John Lombardo, Lopresti's boss, their chop-shop enterprises are escalating. By creating branches up and down the East Coast, Lombardo took a local operation and made it statewide. He upped the ante. His mistake was establishing his business here in Paradise."

"Why is that," Suitcase said.

"Because Paradise is my turf," Jesse said.

They were silent for a while.

"So how was holding Lopresti preemptive," Suitcase said.

"He led us to Lombardo."

"And?"

"We're going to put Lombardo out of business."

"How do you do that?"

"Carefully."

"Come on, Jesse. I'm trying to learn from you. What are you going to do?"

"I'm going to exceed my authority."

"In what way?"

"I'm not going to tell you."

"Why?"

"Because then you'll have deniability in

the event you're questioned."

"You're gonna do what you're gonna do alone," Suitcase said.

"Yes."

"And it won't be legal."

"Correct."

"How do you know what you're going to do will work?"

"I'm the police chief. I know everything."

Suitcase stared at Jesse for a while.

Then Jesse paid for breakfast, and they drove back to Paradise.

33

After an early-morning jog, Jesse fed the cat and made some coffee, which he brought outside to the porch. He settled himself on the love seat to read the paper.

The story of the fire was now old news. Apart from the article regarding safety tips for protecting your dog at night, there was nothing further on the killings. He was about to turn to the sports pages when the cat jumped onto his lap.

He could feel the cat's sharp claws as it made mittens on his leg. He petted it. It began to purr. They stayed that way for some time.

Jesse noticed the two men as soon as he came out of the pet store lugging his newly acquired cat case.

One of them was leaning against a light pole. The other was lounging against a wall. Although each was as wide as he was tall, their upper torsos were raging with steroid-enhanced musculature. Jesse put the case down.

The one closest to him, the wall leaner, walked toward him.

"Mr. Lombardo wants to see you," he said.

"I don't know any Mr. Lombardo," Jesse said.

"Makes no matter. You gonna come with us."

"Gosh, boys, I'd really love to, but I'm afraid I have other plans."

"Hey, you hear that, Frank? Guy says he's got other plans."

The two goons began to laugh.

Jesse stepped quickly to the talker and kicked him hard in the balls. The guy looked at Jesse for half a moment, then went down, gasping for breath.

Before Frank could extricate himself from the light pole, Jesse had smashed the bridge of his nose with the edge of his hand. He stepped quickly aside as Frank started to bleed.

"My nose," he said, his hands flying to his face in order to gingerly explore the fractured remains of his nose.

Jesse turned to goon number one, the talker, lying in a fetal position on the ground.

"Nice work, boys," he said, as he picked up the cat case and walked to his car.

"Zenith Enterprises," Healy said, using his cell phone.

"I'm listening," Jesse said.

"Registered under the name of Geoffrey Bedard, a Boston-based attorney whose specialty is corporate law. Which he practices on behalf of certain underworld organizations. Zenith Enterprises is a repository for a number of corporate entities. I'd venture to guess that upon closer scrutiny of these entities, we'd most likely find considerable sums appearing and disappearing like so many magician's rabbits."

"Signifying?"

"Laundering would be my guess."

"So not only is Lombardo selling stolen goods, he's finding ways to hide the proceeds as well."

"Looks like it."

"Connected to our friend Mr. Fish?"

"My guys are saying that although they make a public show of solidarity, there's no love lost between Gino and Lombardo. Lombardo muscled his way from Fall River to Boston and is brazenly making a play for greater position. He appears to be posing a threat to Gino."

"Are the Feds interested?"

"Interested but inert."

"Because?"

"The story is still unfolding. They have no wish to step on it."

Jesse didn't say anything.

"The information you've uncovered won't sit well with John Lombardo. He thinks of himself as an invisible man. You've succeeded in rending his cloak of invisibility."

"Rending his cloak of invisibility?"

"Has a nice ring to it, don't you think?"

"Thanks for this."

"Service is our middle name," Healy said.

Jesse was on the porch, carefully removing a pane of glass from the floor-to-ceiling French door, which consisted of eight separate panes. He was extricating the bottom-right pane. The cat was perched on the love seat, watching him intently.

He had used a bezel to trim his way around the frame. He had secured the glass with a suction cup, which, when he had completed cutting, he used to pop out the pane.

He then attached a fringed rubber veil to the inside of the window frame, thereby covering the opening.

He looked at the cat, who had been looking at him. He walked to the love seat and picked it up. Remarkably, the cat allowed him to do this. Jesse took the cat to the window and showed him the opening. Then he shoved the cat through the rubber veil and into the house.

The cat immediately turned around and jumped back out.

"Point made," Jesse said to the cat, who was now at the far end of the porch, bathing.

34

At two a.m., Jesse got out of his Explorer, which was parked down the street from John Lombardo's house. He walked to the house and rang the bell.

After a moment an upstairs light went on. Jesse had only a short wait until he saw a downstairs light and heard someone approaching the door. It opened only as far as the security chain would allow. Jesse was standing in the shadows.

"It's the middle of the fucking night," John Lombardo said. "Who are you? What do you want?"

Jesse could see that Lombardo was wearing a bathrobe and slippers, and was unarmed.

"Neighborhood watch," Jesse said. "A patrol officer notified us that a suspicious-looking person was seen in the vicinity of your house. We want to confirm that nothing here is awry."

"There's been no disturbance here," Lombardo said.

"May I look inside to make certain that you're under no coercion, sir?"

"Do I look like I'm under coercion?"

"My instructions are to make certain that you're not being held against your will, sir. There have been other incidents in this neighborhood. If you'll allow me to see that you're safe, I'll be on my way. If not, I'm to phone for backup."

"All right, all right," Lombardo said.

He closed the door, unchained it, and then reopened it so that Jesse could see inside.

Jesse hit him low, taking his legs out from under him. Lombardo crashed heavily to the floor.

"What the fuck . . ." Lombardo said.

"You wanted to see me," Jesse said, as he stood Lombardo up and slammed him into the wall.

"You dare to break into my house? My house," Lombardo said.

"Insolent of me, isn't it," Jesse said. "Why did you send the two goons?"

"What in the fuck do you think you're doing? Do you have any idea who I am?"

"Listen to me, fat boy," Jesse said. "One of your associates killed a man in Paradise over a stolen car. I hold you responsible for that killing. Let this be your warning. If you or any of your meatballs show up in Paradise again, I'll kill you."

Lombardo glared at Jesse.

Jesse smacked him hard in the mouth. Blood appeared on his lower lip.

"Do I make myself clear?"

"You'll pay for this," Lombardo said.

Jesse smacked him again.

"Do I make myself clear?"

Lombardo mumbled his assent.

Jesse stared at him for several moments.

Then he walked to the door, opened it, and left the house.

35

The next morning, Jesse pulled his cruiser to a stop in front of a commercial building located in the north side of Boston. He parked in front of a fire hydrant and went inside.

He approached the receptionist's desk, where he was greeted by a handsome young man wearing a double-breasted blue blazer and a freshly ironed pair of blue jeans. His powder-blue sport shirt was open at the neck. He eyed Jesse warily.

"I'm here to see Gino Fish," Jesse said.

"Do you have an appointment?"

"No."

"Mr. Fish isn't in."

"And if I had an appointment?"

"Who knows."

"What's your name?"

"Steven. What's yours?"

"Jesse."

"Do you have a last name, Jesse?"

"Stone."

"Does Mr. Fish know you?"

"Why don't you ask him?"

"Because he's not in."

"Look, Steven, this is an old game. You say Mr. Fish isn't in. I ask you to tell him I'm here. Again, you say he isn't in."

"I'm following you so far."

"But here's where it gets complicated, so pay close attention. My next line is: If you don't go inside and tell Mr. Fish that I'm waiting to see him, I'm going to call the state homicide commander, who will in turn send ten squad cars packed with dozens of police personnel right to this very door."

"Why didn't you say so?"

"Can we move this along now, Steven?"

"Jesse Stone, yes?"

"Yes."

"I'll be right back."

Steven buzzed himself into Gino's inner sanctum. Jesse meandered around the office, looking at the various paintings and sculptures that were on display there.

Steven returned.

"Mr. Fish is in," he said.

As Jesse brushed past Steven on his way inside, he punched him lightly on the shoulder.

"Some fun, huh," he said.

■ ■ ■ ■

Gino was seated at his desk, thumbing through a sheaf of papers. Behind him, leaning against a wall, listening through a pair of earbuds to a minuscule iPod, stood Vinnie Morris.

Jesse approached the desk and waited. When he came to the end of a page, Gino looked up at him.

"Jesse Stone," he said, his face breaking into a crooked grin.

"Ta-da," Jesse said.

Jesse looked at Vinnie, who nodded to him.

"Sit down, Jesse Stone," Gino said. "It's so rare we have visitors to our little chapel. What brings you?"

"The force of your personality."

"It is forceful, isn't it? But then again, so is yours. Or at least that's what I'm hearing."

Jesse didn't say anything.

"It's amazing to me how deeply you manage to piss people off," Gino said.

"It's a gift," Jesse said.

"One that keeps giving," Gino said.

"Can we quit speaking in tongues, Gino? This associate of yours has become a major nuisance."

"I'm listening."

"He not only set up shop in my backyard, but he killed someone in the process. I sent him a warning, which he appears to have ignored. Now it's become personal."

"I would surmise that the feelings are mutual."

"This stops now, Gino."

"That may be beyond my control."

"It's not beyond mine."

"What do you want from me?"

"Neutrality."

Vinnie Morris appeared not to be listening, but Jesse knew otherwise. Vinnie met Jesse's gaze with one of his own.

"I'm going to force the issue," Jesse said.

"How uncharacteristic of you."

"It may not be pretty."

Gino took a cigar from the box on his desk. He offered one to Jesse. They both unwrapped their cigars. Jesse held his out for Gino to clip. Gino did so. He flicked his lighter and held it to Jesse's cigar. Then he fired up his own.

The two men smoked in silence.

"You're telling me this because . . ." Gino said.

"Because I like you."

"I'm flattered," Gino said.

Then he stood up and nodded to Vinnie Morris.

"It was nice seeing you, Jesse Stone," he said.

Vinnie Morris escorted Jesse to the door. Jesse turned back to Gino.

"Thanks for the cigar," he said.

"Don't mention it," Gino said.

Vinnie saw him out.

36

It was late afternoon and Jesse was nearing Paradise on his way back from Boston when his cell phone rang.

"We've got a hostage situation at the junior high school," Molly said.

"Tell me," Jesse said.

"What we know is that an eighth-grader, a girl, has taken the principal hostage. She has a gun and is threatening to shoot."

"I'm on my way," Jesse said.

He turned on his siren and his light bar, and pressed heavily on the accelerator.

By the time he arrived at the junior high, several members of the Paradise police force were already there. He found Suitcase at the main entrance. The two men went inside the building.

"Talk to me," Jesse said.

"Fourteen-year-old girl," Suit said. "She's in Mrs. Nelson's office with her."

"Anyone else?"

"No," Suit said. "Classes were finished for the day. There were very few people in the building."

"Who else knows?"

"We've kept it under wraps, Jesse. I know how you feel about the media."

"Good work, Suit. Take me to the office."

"You gonna go in?"

"Yes."

"Girl's got a gun."

"She got a name?"

"Lisa Barry."

Jesse stood at the door to Eleanor Nelson's office. He knocked on it.

"Lisa," he said. "This is Police Chief Stone."

After several moments, the girl answered.

"Go away," she said.

"May I come in?"

"I've got a gun."

"I heard," Jesse said.

"I'm not afraid to use it."

"May I come in? I want to talk with you."

"I don't want to talk. If you come in, I'll shoot the bitch."

"At least give me a chance."

"Why should I?"

"Maybe I can help."

"That's a laugh."

"I'm not here to harm you, Lisa. At least

hear me out. If you still feel the same way after, then you can shoot."

"Like you won't try to take the gun away from me," Lisa said.

"I give you my promise that I will come in unarmed and not make any attempt to take your gun."

"Why should I trust you?"

"Because I'm the police chief and I want to help you," Jesse said.

Lisa didn't say anything.

"Give me a chance, Lisa. I'm not your enemy."

After a beat, she said, "Okay."

Jesse cautiously opened the door. He stepped slowly into the room. He nudged the door closed with his foot. He held his hands in the air.

"No gun. See," he said.

Lisa was in front of the principal's desk. She was holding what looked to be a Cobra Derringer automatic. It was pointed at Mrs. Nelson.

Eleanor Nelson was in her mid-forties. She wore a plain gray suit. Medium-length drab brown hair framed her long, pale face, which was marred by two raw-looking scratches.

"Are you all right, Mrs. Nelson," Jesse said.

170

Mrs. Nelson nodded.

Jesse turned to Lisa.

"What's this about, Lisa," he said.

"This bitch doesn't deserve to live. I'm going to kill her."

Lisa leaned across the desk and pressed the pistol into the side of Mrs. Nelson's head. She raked it along her cheek, causing the woman to cringe.

"Bitch," Lisa shouted, in Mrs. Nelson's face.

"Talk to me, Lisa. Tell me why you're doing this," Jesse said.

"Because she's a bitch."

Jesse looked at Lisa. Fourteen. Not yet womanly. Slender. Resolute. Stressed.

"Can you tell me what happened," he said.

Lisa relaxed somewhat. She lowered the pistol and moved back.

"She wouldn't listen. I told her."

"You told her what?"

"About the girls."

"What about the girls?"

"How they ragged on me. How they wouldn't leave me alone."

"Which girls?"

"The Lincoln Village girls. The clique," Lisa said.

"What about the Lincoln Village girls?"

"They're like a gang. They think they're

171

better than everybody. They only talk to themselves. They bully people."

"How do they bully people?"

"They torture them. They gang up on them. They punch them."

"Did they punch you?"

"Yes. They would wait for me. After school. Sometimes before school."

"And?"

"And they would take turns smacking me around," Lisa said.

"How often did this happen?"

"A lot. Sometimes every day. I told this bitch about it, and she did nothing."

"You told Mrs. Nelson?"

"Yes."

Jesse turned to the principal. "Did she tell you about this?"

"She accosted me in the parking lot one afternoon and started telling me about some girls who were bullying her," Mrs. Nelson said.

"And?"

"I told her that the parking lot was not the place to discuss it."

"You didn't talk to her?"

"I told her to make an appointment to see me."

"Lisa, is this what happened?"

"She said, 'Not now.' Then she got in her

car and drove away."

"Did she ask you to make an appointment to see her," Jesse said.

"She might have."

"Did you make an appointment with her?"

"Her assistant told me the bitch was too busy to see me. She told me to talk to my homeroom teacher."

"Do you often see students with problems, Mrs. Nelson?"

"On occasion."

"Were you aware that Lisa was trying to make an appointment with you?"

"No."

"An upset student accosts you in a parking lot. You tell her to make an appointment. None is made. Did you wonder why?"

"I'm very busy, Chief Stone. I don't remember ever thinking of the incident again."

"Did you speak with your homeroom teacher, Lisa," Jesse said.

"Yeah, right. Like that dipshit would give me the time of day."

"So you didn't speak with her?"

"Him. Mr. Tauber. He doesn't give a shit about me. He only cares about the Lincoln Village girls. They sit on his lap."

Jesse looked at Mrs. Nelson, who looked away.

"So you didn't actually speak with anyone about the Lincoln Village girls?"

"I tried to speak with her again," Lisa said, pointing at Mrs. Nelson. "Things had gotten worse. They were beating me up every day. Sometimes twice a day."

Jesse didn't say anything.

"So I waited after school. In the hall. When Miss Shit-for-Brains here came out, I tried to tell her. Again, she wouldn't listen."

"Is this true, Mrs. Nelson?"

"She may have tried to talk with me. I can't remember. There are so many things . . ."

"Did you tell your parents about this, Lisa," Jesse said.

"My mom's dead. My dad works all the time."

"So you didn't actually tell any grown-up about what was going on?"

"No. It was so bad I wanted to kill myself. I even stole my dad's gun. This one. Then I thought I'd kill this bitch instead."

She raised the gun and waved it at Mrs. Nelson.

"I understand, Lisa," Jesse said.

"Yeah, good. So you gonna do anything about it," Lisa said. "Or are you gonna turn out to be just like this dirtbag?"

"I'm going to do something about it."

Lisa didn't say anything.

"Do you believe me?"

"I'd like to believe you."

"Will you give me the gun, Lisa? No one's going to hurt you again. I promise."

Lisa looked at Jesse. After a while she lowered the gun. Mrs. Nelson took a deep breath. Jesse walked to Lisa and held out his hand. She put the pistol in it. He checked the safety. He pocketed it.

Then he reached out to her. He gently touched her shoulder.

"I'm sorry this happened, Lisa," he said.

Tears started to fall from her eyes.

He hugged her until the sobbing stopped.

With his arm around her, Jesse and Lisa left the office. They went outside and walked slowly to his cruiser. He opened the passenger-side door for her. She got in.

Jesse made eye contact with Suitcase.

Then he got in the cruiser and drove away.

37

Jesse drove Lisa to the station. Together they went inside. After settling her in the conference room, he went looking for Molly.

When he found her, he told her what had happened. He asked her to sit with Lisa. To take down her story. He wanted the names of each of the Lincoln Village girls. He also asked her to check with Suitcase to see if the girl's father had been found. He walked with her to the conference room.

On the way, Molly mentioned that Rich Bauer had phoned.

"And," he said.

"Two more Hondas were stolen."

"Not a good sign."

"I thought you might say that."

"Look after Lisa. She needs some TLC."

"I don't remember administering TLC as being part of the job description."

"You don't fool me," Jesse said.

"I don't fool you how?"

"You're a softie. Mush."

"Mush?"

"You heard me."

"That's not how I like to think of myself."

"How do you like to think of yourself?"

"Hard. Tough. Terrifying."

"Works for me," Jesse said.

"And the mush?"

"Side dish."

"Just so we don't confuse a side dish with the main course," she said, as she went into the conference room.

Jesse poured some coffee. He phoned Dr. Phyllis Canter, a child psychologist who lived in Paradise. He told her what had happened and asked if she might interview Lisa. She agreed to stop by the station and speak with her.

He stuck his head in the conference room. He explained to Lisa that Dr. Canter would be stopping by. He said he would see her later.

He left the station and headed for his cruiser, which was parked in its designated spot behind the building.

He only noticed the movement out of the corner of his eye. A man was rapidly approaching Jesse from behind a double-parked car. He was holding a pistol.

177

Jesse dove to the ground just as the man fired. He pulled his pistol from its holster. It was in his hand with the safety off before he hit the ground.

He got off two quick shots, the first of which struck his assailant in the chest.

Jesse rolled into a sitting position and fired three more times.

The double-parked sedan sped away, tires screeching. Jesse fired at it.

Then he stood, and with his pistol extended, walked toward the man lying on the ground. He knelt beside him and felt for a pulse. There was none.

Jesse holstered his pistol just as Suitcase and Steve Lesnick burst from the station house, their service weapons in their hands.

Jesse signaled to them that there was no longer a threat. They put their weapons away.

"See if he has ID on him," Jesse said to Suitcase.

To Steve Lesnick he said, "There's a late-model sedan which just left the parking lot in a big hurry. I think it was a Buick. I couldn't get the license. Maybe there's someone who can track it."

Suitcase searched the body.

Lesnick reached for his cell phone.

"Nothing, Jesse," Suitcase said. "Not even

a wallet. What do you make of it?"

"Mob hit," Jesse said. "Secure the scene. Call for a CSI unit. Let me know if anyone spots the getaway vehicle."

As Jesse walked back to the station, the two officers looked at each other.

"I was right," Lesnick said.

"About what," Suitcase said.

"About Jesse," Lesnick said.

"What about Jesse," Suitcase said.

"He didn't even flinch. It's like he's got ice water for blood."

"Tell me something I don't know," Suitcase said.

Once inside, Jesse took a couple of deep breaths. He realized how narrowly he had escaped being shot. He knew the hit was the work of John Lombardo.

Jesse reached for the phone and called Gino Fish.

"Your dime," Gino said.

"Remember our discussion about neutrality?"

"I'm listening," Gino said.

"We need to revisit the subject."

"Something personal?"

"We need to talk."

"I shall look forward to it, Jesse Stone," Gino said.

■ ■ ■ ■

When Phyllis Canter had finished interviewing Lisa Barry, she stuck her head into Jesse's office. She was a pleasant-looking woman of indeterminate age. Her mouth curled with a hint of a smile. Her rich brown eyes sparkled with intelligence. He stood to greet her.

"Phyllis," he said.

"Hello, Jesse," she said.

"How's Lisa?"

"Better than I would have expected. She's motivated by anger. Very likely misplaced, however."

"Meaning?"

"May I speak shrink talk?"

"Only if you'll provide a running translation," Jesse said.

Dr. Canter smiled.

"Her anger is directed at her mother. For having died and abandoned her. She hasn't dealt with that anger. Nor with her grief, either. I'd like to see her some more. I can help her."

"When I see her father, I'll talk to him about it," Jesse said. "He's not picking up his cell. I'm gonna track him down."

"The father may very well be an emotional

cretin. You need to make certain he doesn't stand in the way. You'll have to be at your persuasive best."

"One emotional cretin to another," Jesse said.

"I didn't want to bring it up," Dr. Canter said.

In the late afternoon, Jesse drove Lisa to her father's office. She had mentioned that he rarely came home until late. Sometimes even after she had gone to bed.

"How did you like Dr. Canter," Jesse said.

"She's all right," Lisa said.

"What did you talk about?"

"Stuff."

"Do you want to tell me?"

"Not really."

"Do you want to see her again?"

"Yes. Maybe. Yes."

"So you liked her?"

"She was all right," Lisa said.

They arrived at Leonard Barry's office, which was located in a small warehouse on the outskirts of town. Barry was involved in some sort of import/export enterprise. A panel truck with his name painted on it was parked out front. Lisa led the way inside.

"What are you doing here," her father said, when he saw her. "Who's this?"

"Jesse Stone," Jesse said. "Paradise chief of police."

"I heard of you," Leonard Barry said. "What can I do for you?"

He was looking at Lisa, who was looking at the floor. Jesse told him everything that had transpired at the school. He also mentioned Dr. Canter.

"Is Lisa under arrest," Mr. Barry said.

"No," Jesse said.

"Because?"

"Because arresting her wouldn't be the right thing to do. Lisa has been the victim of considerable abuse. What she did, she did in self-defense."

"So what do you want from me?"

"Parental responsibility."

Lisa was sitting quietly, looking at her father, listening. Her father occasionally looked at her.

"You think I'm not a responsible parent," Leonard Barry said.

"This incident might be an indicator."

"I work my ass off so that she can have what she needs."

"What she needs is you involved in her life," Jesse said.

"I am involved in her life."

"Maybe. Maybe not. Did you know she was dealing with some serious issues?"

"She never said anything."

"Perhaps she never had the chance."

"What's that supposed to mean?"

"If you're not around to listen, how can she tell you anything? Responsible parenting means being present and available. Being attuned to all of the signals."

Mr. Barry didn't say anything.

"Lisa showed up at school today with your pistol," Jesse said. "Did you know she had it? That she not only threatened the principal's life with it but her own life as well? That's a big signal to have missed."

Mr. Barry looked down.

"Lisa is still reeling from the loss of her mother, which is trauma enough. It also seems as if she's lost her father as well. Something's not right here."

Mr. Barry didn't say anything.

"Perhaps you could talk with her about what's been going on in her life," Jesse said. "And maybe pay close attention to what she has to say. There's nothing more important for either of you."

Mr. Barry looked up.

Jesse stood.

"I'm gonna have a talk with the Lincoln Village girls tomorrow," he said.

"You are," Lisa said.

"I am."

"Wow," she said.

38

Jesse couldn't sleep. His mind was on overload, which finally drove him out of bed and downstairs, where he fixed himself a scotch.

When he brought it into the living room, he was surprised to find the cat asleep on one of his two leather armchairs. It barely raised its head when Jesse sat down in the chair next to it.

Jesse took a sip and smiled. He had become attached to the cat. Or, more likely, he was now owned by it. Which gave him purpose. He put his feet up and continued to sip the scotch.

He had narrowly avoided being killed today. And in turn, he had killed a man. The fact of which had barely registered amid the chaos of the day. The man was still unidentified and lay on a slab at the morgue.

A life, thought Jesse. *A man's life. Given up*

in the service of what? Defending the interests of some psychopath?

He thought about Lisa Barry. Alone. Bullied by a group of privileged adolescents who were acting out psychological issues that probably had nothing to do with her. Rebuffed by a desensitized authority figure. Begging for parental attention.

He thought about the odd series of events that had been plaguing Paradise. Animal killings. Arson.

What am I missing, he asked himself. *What's the connection?*

He considered Alexis Richardson. What was he doing with her? He had pushed Sunny Randall away. He had permanently shut the door on Jenn. He was just beginning to feel comfortable being alone. Now, suddenly, there was Alexis. Why?

Songs from the past kept running through his mind. Songs about summer love, summer romance. He was having a summer fling is what he was doing. With apparently no strings attached. Maybe.

What's the connection, he asked himself again.

An unfamiliar noise registered in his now somewhat sodden consciousness. Something outside.

He picked up his Colt Commander and

his Smith & Wesson tactical high-beam flashlight. He opened the porch door and went outside. He stood there, listening. Then he switched on the flashlight and began a slow tour of his grounds. He circled the house. He didn't detect anything strange. He went back inside.

He sipped the last of the scotch.

What's the connection, he said again.

Finally, he turned off the lights and went upstairs to bed.

After a while, Rollo dared to move. He carefully climbed out of the thorn bushes in which he had been hiding. He looked at the darkened house.

"Dead man walking," he said.

Then he crossed the footbridge and hurried away.

39

War Memorial Park was fairly deserted. A couple of joggers, a dog walker. Jesse sat, staring at the memorial statue. It was meant to be a postmodern version of the *Winged Victory,* but to his eye, it was a steel-and-concrete disaster. A waste of what he surmised had been significant funding.

Gino Fish sat next to him, also looking at the statue.

"Atrocious," he said.

"Worse than that," Jesse said.

"May I tell you a story, Jesse Stone," Gino said.

"As long as it begins with 'Once upon a time,' " Jesse said.

"It begins with a killing."

"I don't like killings," Jesse said.

"This particular killing, however, brought a certain minor player out of obscurity and into the spotlight. He must have been blinded by it, because instead of retreating from it, he embraced it. He started to behave erratically. He reached for the stars, so to speak. Are you following me so far, Jesse Stone?"

"It's hard, but I'm doing my best," Jesse said.

"In no time, the player began to wear out his welcome. He overstepped his bounds. His friends began to shy away from him. Soon he stood alone. He had become expendable."

"This is a very sad story," Jesse said.

"For the player, it is."

Gino didn't say any more.

"Is that the end," Jesse said.

"Almost," Gino said.

The two men sat silently for a while, staring at the statue.

40

Jesse arrived at the junior high school and headed directly to Eleanor Nelson's office. He told her he wanted to interview the four Lincoln Village girls. She told him to wait in the conference room.

Once there, Jesse opened the file Molly had prepared. It contained the identities of each of the girls as well as brief descriptions of them and their families.

One by one the girls began to file in. After they were all present, Jesse closed the door and sat down at the conference table across from them.

"I'm Jesse Stone," he said. "The police chief of Paradise. Thank you for joining me."

He asked each of them their names. They nervously told him.

One of the girls, Julie Knoller, appeared to be the ringleader. She was pre-punk. She wore a black T-shirt and heavily studded black jeans. Her eyes were lined in black.

All that was missing were the piercings, which would surely come when she was older.

"I asked you here because it has come to my attention that you have been behaving in a manner unbecoming of young ladies and have been disrespectful of the rights of other students. Do you know what I'm talking about?"

"No," Julie Knoller said.

"You don't know what I'm talking about?"

"No."

"Do you know a girl named Lisa Barry?"

"No," Julie Knoller said.

"This isn't going well," Jesse said. None of the girls said anything.

"Let me start over," he said. "We're having this conversation because I didn't want to arrest you and create a brouhaha involving your parents and the district attorney and lawyers and a whole lot of grief. This state has anti-bullying laws, which you have violated. If you continue to be uncooperative, I will arrest you and place you in the criminal justice system, and things will become much more difficult for you."

The girls began to fidget and to exchange nervous glances with one another.

"Do you understand why we're having this conversation," he said to Julie Knoller.

"I guess," she finally admitted.

"Do you know a girl named Lisa Barry?"

Julie nodded.

None of the other girls would look at Jesse.

"Did you repeatedly attack her?"

Jesse looked at one of the girls.

"What's your name again," he said.

"Lesly Berson," she said.

"What have you got against Lisa Barry, Lesly?"

Lesly shrugged.

"Answer the question."

"We didn't like her, okay," Lesly said.

"You didn't like her enough to beat the crap out of her on a regular basis?"

She shrugged.

"Answer me," Jesse said.

Lesly looked around the table at the other girls.

"We all decided that she'd be the one."

"She'd be the one what?"

"The one we'd hammer."

"Because?"

"She was a loser. She didn't have any friends. She pissed us off."

Jesse looked at one of the other girls.

"Tell me your name," he said.

"Shauna Hatt," the girl said.

"Did Lisa ever do anything to you, Shauna," Jesse said.

"I don't know."

"You don't know," Jesse said.

"She was a jerk."

"That's why you ganged up on her?"

"She acted like a retard," Bonnie Wilder said.

"She didn't have a mother," Shauna said.

"It felt good to beat her up," Julie said. "She was so pathetic."

"Let me get this straight," Jesse said. "Lisa was friendless. You thought she was pathetic. You knew her mother was dead, yet instead of showing compassion, you chose to regularly kick the shit out of her. What's wrong with this picture?"

"Well, when you put it that way . . ." Shauna said.

"You bullied and harassed this girl to the point where she was contemplating suicide. Did you know that?"

"Know what," Julie said.

"That she planned to kill herself," Jesse said.

"She did," Bonnie said.

"There was a case in the news recently where a group of schoolgirls, not unlike yourselves, continually harassed another girl. So unrelentingly that the girl finally committed suicide. When it came out that they had been bullying the dead girl, these girls were arrested and indicted, and stood trial for second-degree murder. They all face jail time. Their lives have been ruined. Is that what you want for yourselves?"

The girls looked at one another. A couple of them shook their heads.

"Did you ever think that there might be consequences for your behavior?"

"We were just fucking with her," Julie said.

"She asked for it," Lesly said.

"Do you feel any remorse for your behavior," Jesse said.

"Why should we," Bonnie said.

The girls all looked at each other.

"How do you think your parents will feel when they find out about this?"

"They won't care," Julie said.

"What happens between you and your parents is between you and them. What happens between you and me is what I'm interested in," Jesse said. "Stop harassing Lisa Barry. And anyone else you may have been bullying. Okay? If you don't, there will be consequences. You'll face prosecution. You'll face jail time. And I will personally make each of your lives hell. Do you understand me?"

The girls nodded.

"I will instruct each of you to undergo psychological counseling. It's important that you understand what you brought upon yourselves and why."

"Psychological counseling," Bonnie Wilder said.

"With a proper shrink," Jesse said.

The girls were quiet.

Jesse stood and began to walk around the table, looking directly at each of them.

"I'm going to haunt you," he said. "One slip, one more incident, and you'll regret it for the rest of your lives. Do I make myself clear?"

No one spoke.

"Do I make myself clear?"

Jesse stared at each girl until she answered.

"You're going to start by apologizing to Lisa Barry. A sincere apology, too. No bullshit. You will regard her as a person. Say hello to her when it's warranted. Treat her as you would want to be treated. Is that clear," Jesse said.

Under Jesse's gaze, each girl nodded again.

"Good," Jesse said.

He walked to the door.

"Have a nice day, ladies," he said, as he left.

On his way out, Jesse stopped by Eleanor Nelson's office. She stood as he entered.

"Chief Stone," she said.

"Mrs. Nelson," Jesse said. "I want you to know that my response to what I learned yesterday has not been good."

"Meaning?"

"Meaning that I believe you violated your position and brought shame on your office."

Mrs. Nelson looked down.

"I'm going to launch an investigation into Mr. Tauber's behavior. If I find that he has been involved in sexual misconduct of any nature, I'll make certain that he is prosecuted to the full extent of the law."

Mrs. Nelson didn't say anything.

"I want you to think of how your expressed indifference impacted the life of an already unsettled young woman," Jesse said. "Your priorities are fucked, Mrs. Nelson, if you'll pardon my French. The responsibility you hold for the well-being of the young people in your charge is paramount. Of greater importance than anything else. If there's any possible way that I can separate you from your job, you can bet your ass that I'm going to find it. Shame on you, madam."

Jesse turned and left. He resisted the impulse to slam the door behind him.

41

Jesse stood to greet Gino Fish as he was ushered to their table at Il Capriccio.

"Your server will be along shortly to take your drink order," the maître d' said, and then scurried away.

Gino looked around the restaurant.

"Your first time," Jesse said.

"Yes. Yours?"

"No," Jesse said. "I actually learned the identity of John Lombardo here."

"Ah," Gino said. "Once we select our wine, we must surely offer a toast to him."

"May I ask you a dumb question," Jesse said.

"There's no such thing as a dumb question, Jesse Stone," Gino said.

"Why are we here," Jesse said.

"I thought that's what you might ask," Gino said.

"So?"

"Let's just say that it's in both of our

interests to be seen together tonight."

"May I ask a follow-up question?"

"Not just now," Gino said, as the server stopped by with the wine list.

It was shortly after seven o'clock and raining when Vinnie Morris pulled up to Zenith Enterprises. The streets were empty, and he found a parking space directly in front.

He pressed the admittance button on the security panel.

After a moment, a voice filtered through the electronic system.

"Who's there," the voice said.

"Vinnie Morris."

The door opened. A simian-looking creature dressed in a jacket and tie greeted Vinnie.

"Yo, Vinnie," the man said.

"Vito," Vinnie said. "Boss wants five minutes with Mr. Lombardo."

"We was just closin' up. Lemme go tell him."

Vinnie stepped inside. Vito closed the door behind him.

Vito headed for John Lombardo's office.

Once there, he pressed three numbers into the security panel beside the door. The latch released, and the door sprang open.

Vito looked back at Vinnie.

"I'll tell the boss," he said.

Vinnie suddenly drew his pistol and shot Vito twice in the heart. With a look of astonishment on his face, Vito collapsed, already dead.

Vinnie stepped over the body and entered the office.

Lombardo, having heard the shots, was reaching for the pistol inside his desk when Vinnie approached him.

"What the fuck is this," he said.

"I have a message for you from Gino Fish," Vinnie said.

Lombardo looked up, his eyes bulging.

"Always look on the bright side of life," Vinnie said.

He shot Lombardo in the forehead, the aftermath of which permanently altered the painting of himself that hung on the wall behind his desk.

Vinnie quickly left the office and buzzed himself out of the building. He took a handkerchief from his pocket and wiped down the buzzer, both handles of the door, and the admittance button alongside it.

He looked up and down the street.

Seeing no one, he ducked into his car and drove away.

Jesse and Gino had finished their dinners

and were enjoying an excellent zabaglione. Two spoons.

The restaurant was full, with the sole exception of the large table in the center of the room, which had been set for seven. A "Reserved" sign was on the table, but no one was seated there.

When the server brought the check, Gino waved Jesse off and reached for it. He barely glanced at it. He pulled out a wad of bills from his pocket. He thumbed a number of them from the wad and handed them to the server.

"Keep the change," he said. "We had an excellent dinner. Memorable, even."

"Thank you, sir," the server said. "We hope you'll return."

"I fully intend to," Gino said. "Who's that big table reserved for? Some visiting movie star?"

"Not tonight," the server said with a chuckle. "It's reserved for one of our regulars."

The server glanced at his watch.

"That's odd," he said. "They're late."

"Probably the traffic," Gino said.

The server nodded. Then he picked up the empty dessert plate and hurried away.

Gino looked at Jesse.

"Probably the traffic," he said.

42

Jesse sat amid a group that included twin standard poodles, a miniature schnauzer, and an overweight pit bull whose attention was riveted on the cat case.

Finally, he was admitted to the inner sanctum of Dr. Mary Ann Kennerly, a bustling African American woman widely regarded as the best veterinarian in Paradise.

"This is a first," Dr. Kennerly said. "The chief of police in my office. And from the looks of it, accompanied by a cat."

"It adopted me," Jesse said.

"A lot of that going around," Dr. Kennerly said. "Put it on the examining table, Jesse. Let's have a look."

Jesse opened the top of the carrying case, and the cat gingerly stuck out its head. It looked around, then ducked back in.

"Come on, little one," Dr. Kennerly said. "Nothing bad's gonna happen."

She lifted the cat from the case. She put it on her examining table. She placed her hands on it.

"Young," Dr. Kennerly said. "No more than four or five months. Female."

"Female," Jesse said. "You're sure?"

"You got something against females?"

"No. No. I had come to think of it as a male."

"Think again. Also think about having her spayed."

"Spayed."

"Are you gonna repeat everything I say?"

"Spayed," Jesse said. "As in neutered?"

"Exactly."

"I don't know how I feel about neutering an animal."

"How you feel about it?"

"Shouldn't animals have the same reproductive rights as humans?"

"Absolutely not," Dr. Kennerly said.

"Because?"

"Because the last thing you need are semiannual litters. Too many of these critters are already being euthanized. We don't need to add to that number."

"Well, when you put it that way."

"I perform surgeries on Wednesdays. Make an appointment."

Dr. Kennerly continued her examination.

"Forgive me for asking," she said, "but what's being done about the dog killings?"

"Everything that can be."

"Any progress?"

"Between you and me, Mary Ann, none that I can cite."

"How strange it is."

"Tell me about it."

"If anyone can put a stop to it, it's most assuredly you, Jesse."

"Thanks for the vote of confidence. I can't help but believe that we're gonna catch a break. People are aware of what's going on. Killer is bound to trip up. Sooner rather than later, I'm hoping."

"The good news is this little girl appears to be in excellent condition," the doctor said. "Whatever you're doing, keep doing it. I'll give her a few shots, and when you can, bring her in for the surgery."

"Little girl," Jesse said. "And here I was preparing to take him hunting and fishing with me."

"After the surgery you'll have less trouble keeping the boys away."

"Every father's dream," Jesse said.

Jesse took the cat home, then headed for the office. His cell phone rang.

"Jesse," he said.

"Have you seen the Boston papers," Healy said.

"I live in Paradise," Jesse said.

"I always wondered why you were so ill-informed."

"What am I missing?"

" 'Mobster Murdered.' Headline story in both papers," Healy said.

"Which mobster?"

"Ask that question with a straight face."

"What do the papers think?"

"They concur."

"On what?"

"They agree that Mr. Lombardo was the victim of Mob violence."

"How awful."

"You wouldn't know anything about this, would you," Healy asked.

"About what?"

Healy didn't say anything.

"Did the Sox win," Jesse said.

"I didn't get that far."

"Speaking of the ill-informed," Jesse said.

43

Assistant District Attorney Martin Reagan relaxed in his chair and smiled at his visitor.

"It's so rare that we get to see an actual police chief," Reagan said. "To what do we owe the honor?"

"I wanted to bask in the glow of your greatness," Jesse said.

"Bask all you want," Reagan said. "Just don't touch anything. What brings you to the hallowed halls of justice?"

"An incident that took place at the junior high school. Fourteen-year-old girl took Eleanor Nelson hostage. Held her at gunpoint. On the surface, it would appear as if the girl acted criminally. When you look deeper, however, turns out she was the victim of continued abuse by a gang of other girls. When she reached out to Mrs. Nelson, she was backhandedly dismissed. Kid thought about killing herself. Nearly a repeat of the situation in South Hadley. Kid killed herself because no one stood up for her."

"And you're going to stand up for this kid," Marty Reagan said.

"You bet I am."

Reagan flashed Jesse a smile. Then he said, "Are you thinking you might want to bring charges against the principal?"

"I might be."

"Why?"

"She should be held accountable. She behaved unconscionably."

"You think she broke the law?"

"That's a lawyer question, not a policeman question," Jesse said.

"Was there anything else?"

"Maybe."

"Do you want to tell me about it?"

"Not yet."

"Do you want to give me a hint?"

"There's a likelihood of sexual misconduct on the part of one of the junior high teachers."

"A likelihood?"

"Yes."

"And you're investigating this likelihood," Reagan said.

"Yes."

Reagan sat thinking for several moments.

"Get me the information. I'll work with

you on this, Jesse."

"Thanks, Marty," Jesse said, as he stood up. "It's always a pleasure."

The assistant district attorney stood and reached for Jesse's hand.

"Carole keeps asking when we're going to see you. It's been too long."

"It has. Let me get the season under way. This one promises to be a doozy."

"A doozy?"

"Pretty much."

Jesse was waiting when Stuart Tauber left the junior high school in the late afternoon. Tauber was headed for the parking lot when Jesse intercepted him.

"Mr. Tauber," he said.

Tauber slowed and looked at Jesse. He was soft and overweight, which he tried to conceal behind a houndstooth jacket and baggy slacks. He was pasty-faced, with thinning hair. His eyes darted this way and that, avoiding contact with Jesse's.

"Yes," he said.

"Have you got a moment," Jesse said.

"Only just," Tauber said. "What can I do for you?"

"Jesse Stone," Jesse said.

He didn't extend his hand.

"I know who you are," Tauber said. "Your

reputation precedes you."

"Oh," Jesse said. "What reputation is that?"

"Your serious alcohol-related issues."

"And you know about that because . . ."

"Let's just say that people in a small town have a tendency to talk."

"So that's it, then? That's the talk? My whole reputation?"

"That's not enough," Tauber said.

"What about the good stuff?"

"I beg your pardon?"

"The good stuff. Isn't any good stuff a part of my reputation?"

"I heard you had a smart mouth. Is this an example of it?"

"I don't think you like me, Mr. Tauber."

"For the record, no, I don't like you or what you stand for."

"For the record," Jesse said.

"Was there something you wanted to see me about, Chief Stone?"

"Actually, there was."

"Do you want to tell me about it?"

"I wanted to see who you were."

"Because?"

"Because your reputation precedes you."

"What's that supposed to mean?"

"I think you know what it means."

"I think this conversation is over," Tauber

said, as he started to walk away.

"You're in my sights, Tauber."

"Is that some kind of threat, Stone?"

"It is what it is," Jesse said.

"You keep away from me," Tauber said.

"Is that some kind of threat, Tauber?"

"I'm a respected member of the education community," Tauber said. "I don't take kindly to harassment."

"Harassment?"

"You heard me."

"You've only just begun to hear me, Mr. Tauber," Jesse said.

"Keep away from me, Stone," Tauber said. He hurried off.

Jesse watched him go.

44

"It's a girl," Jesse said.

"Excuse me," Alexis said.

"The cat. It's a girl."

They were sitting on Jesse's porch. The cat was asleep on her lap. Alexis was sipping a vodka and lemonade; Jesse a scotch. They were contemplating dinner.

"Mildred Memory," Jesse said.

"What," Alexis said.

"That's what I named her. Mildred Memory."

"What kind of name is that?"

"It was the name of my favorite high school teacher."

"Mildred Memory?"

"Yes."

"So how exactly will you address the cat?"

"As Mildred Memory."

"You mean you'll say things like 'Here, Mildred Memory.' "

"Exactly."

"Doesn't that seem a bit eccentric?"

"Not to us," said Jesse.

"Us?"

"Mildred Memory and me."

Alexis sipped her drink and didn't say anything.

Jesse didn't say anything.

Mildred Memory didn't say anything.

"I've booked my first festival," Alexis said.

"You have," Jesse said.

"Fourth of July weekend."

"And Uncle Carter has approved?"

"He has."

"Congratulations. What's the show?"

"An all-day rock concert, of course. I booked a whole bunch of bands. July fourth. The high school stadium. The show will start at three o'clock and go for as long as it goes."

"Not past eleven o'clock," Jesse said.

"More likely until two or three."

"Not past eleven o'clock."

"What do you mean?"

"Curfew," Jesse said.

"Curfew?"

"Eleven p.m. Town law. You could look it up."

"Why didn't you mention this before?"

"You never asked."

"That's awful," she said.

211

"Not for the people who live near the stadium," Jesse said.

"Do you think Uncle Carter could get an exception?"

"Not while I'm around."

"Couldn't you look the other way?"

"I don't think you should be asking me that question," Jesse said.

"But this changes everything."

"Why?"

"Becausc concerts like this don't generally end until well after midnight."

"This one will."

"People might not want to attend a concert that ends so early."

"Why not?"

"Because that's when things really start happening."

"You'll have to stop the music at eleven," Jesse said.

"Do you realize how important this is to me, Jesse," Alexis said.

"I do."

"And you won't bend the rules? Even for me?"

"No," Jesse said.

"How can you be so intransigent?"

Jesse didn't say anything.

"What if we don't stop?"

"I'll have to stop it for you."

Alexis looked at Jesse. She put down her drink and stood up.

"You don't give an inch, do you?"

"Not where the law is concerned," Jesse said.

"And where I'm concerned?"

"I've told you where I stand."

"You stand alone," she said, and left.

45

Rollo set the fire in a garbage can that he had taken from a neighboring house. He had lined the can with pieces of newspaper and had added a bundle of kindling wood that he had purchased at the market. He emptied nearly an entire can of lighter fluid over the paper and the wood. He lit it, then melted into the shadows to await the results.

The fire burned for twenty or so minutes before there was any response. Then a silver Chevy sedan pulled up alongside the burning can. A man got out of the sedan and opened the trunk. He grabbed a fire extinguisher and began to spray it on the fire.

Rollo came out of hiding and approached the man from behind. He knew that the man was part of the night patrol on the lookout for the dog killer. He assumed the man was a police officer.

Before the man could react, Rollo grabbed his head in both of his hands and violently twisted it until he heard the man's neck break.

Then he let go, and the man fell to the ground. Rollo watched him die.

Afterward he dragged the man back to his vehicle. He lifted him up and put him inside.

Then he reached inside and popped the Chevy's gas tank cover. He walked to the side of the car and unscrewed the cap.

He placed a string of twisted toilet paper inside the gas tank and unrolled the paper until it stretched to a fair distance away from the car. He doused the paper with lighter fluid. He lit the end of the paper, and as it began to burn its way toward the gas tank, Rollo ran from the car.

He had reached the street corner when he heard the explosion. He turned back in time to see a massive ball of flame erupting from the car. He could feel the heat.

He hugged the shadows and got away as fast as he could.

Jesse was watching the old-movie channel when the phone rang. The movie was *The Graduate,* and it was just getting to the part where Ben disrupted Elaine's wedding.

"Shit," he said, and answered the phone.

"Jesse, it's Rich. We've got a situation."

■ ■ ■ ■

By the time Jesse got to the scene, the fire had been extinguished. The charred remains of the car were still smoldering.

Mickey Kurtz was watching the smoke rise. Rich Bauer stood with him. Jesse walked over to them.

"We've got a body here, Jesse," Kurtz said.

"Who," Jesse said.

"Steve Lesnick was on patrol with me tonight," Bauer said.

"We can't make any positive identification yet," Kurtz said. "But in all likelihood it's Steve."

Jesse stepped away and took a moment to collect himself. He walked to the fire-damaged automobile and looked inside. He gazed at Steve Lesnick's remains. A fellow officer. A friend.

The body was burned beyond recognition. Jesse thought it strange that it was lying on the seat. He looked more closely and saw that the head was tilted at an odd angle. He called to Captain Kurtz.

"Mick," he said. "Have a look at something, will you?"

Kurtz joined him beside the car.

"Look at the angle of the head," Jesse said.

"Odd," Kurtz said. "Almost as if . . ."

". . . Yeah," Jesse said.

"I better have forensics take a closer look," Kurtz said.

"Good idea," Jesse said.

46

The Lesnick funeral was attended by seemingly everyone in Paradise. The crowd overflowed the church. Many of the attendees listened to the service over a loudspeaker that had been placed on the sidewalk.

It wasn't the first time that a Paradise police officer had been killed in the line of duty. But it was the first time Jesse had worn his uniform.

"Steve would have loved that you attended in uniform," Molly said.

"Especially my discomfort," Jesse said.

He and Molly were outside the church, looking around.

Jesse spotted Alexis Richardson standing with Carter Hansen. He and Alexis hadn't spoken since the night of Steve's death. Which was also the night they'd fought.

After the service, following a brief moment spent with the Lesnick family, Jesse joined the crowd as it made its way out of the church. He caught up with Alexis. She looked at him but said nothing.

"Sad day," he said.

"He was your friend," she said.

"He was," Jesse said.

"Uncle Carter says he was a good cop."

"He was."

"I'm sorry for your loss."

"Thank you."

They walked together for a ways.

"Don't think you can make up with me, Jesse," she said.

"You're not still angry, are you," Jesse said.

"Of course I'm still angry."

"Surely you're not going to hold me responsible for a matter which is essentially out of my hands," Jesse said.

"That's not what my uncle thinks."

"Hansen told you it would be all right to play amplified music for as long as you like?"

"Something like that, yes."

"Then he's misstating the law."

"Or interpreting it differently than you," Alexis said.

"There's no interpretation required. The town rules are eminently clear."

"Apparently not to Selectman Hansen."

"Does that mean you plan on defying the law?"

"This country was built upon people defying the law," Alexis said.

"So you are planning to defy it."

"I didn't say that."

"You didn't have to."

"Don't get in my way, Jesse."

"I don't particularly appreciate that remark."

"There's no appreciation required," she said.

"That's what you think," Jesse said.

He glared at her for a few minutes.

Then he walked away.

47

"You came to see me for information," Dix said.

"Yes," Jesse said.

"Not for treatment."

"Yes."

"What kind of information?"

"I'm not certain."

"You came to me for information, but you're not certain what information you came for?"

"Yes."

"Again with the one-word answers."

"You used to be a cop, right?"

"Right."

"Did you ever experience serial behavior," Jesse said.

"You mean like the behavior behind the killings and the fires?"

"Yes."

"No."

"No you didn't experience this kind of

behavior," Jesse said.

"Yes," Dix said.

Jesse didn't say anything.

"Serial behavior comes in all sizes," Dix said. "What you're dealing with seems to be coming in all sizes at once."

"Which means?"

"It takes many shapes, but it seems to have one objective."

"Which is?"

"My guess is that it's aimed at you personally," Dix said.

"At me?"

"Exactly."

"Because?"

"You tell me."

Jesse didn't say anything.

Dix didn't say anything.

Jesse suddenly blurted the name: "Rollo Nurse."

"Bingo," Dix said.

"You knew it was Rollo Nurse?"

"I wasn't certain."

"I kept circling, but I couldn't pin it down," Jesse said.

"It became clear the instant you blurted it out," Dix said.

Jesse didn't say anything.

"It makes sense," Dix said.

"It does," Jesse said. "I couldn't make the

connection."

"Now you have."

"He killed Steve Lesnick."

"Killed?"

"Broke his neck before he set fire to the car," Jesse said.

"What are you gonna do?"

"I'm gonna take him down."

"Which means?"

"I'm going to find him and apprehend him."

"And if you can't successfully do that," Dix said.

"Then I'll kill him."

"Just as you feared."

48

When Julie Knoller meandered onto Sixth Street in Lincoln Village, she thought it odd that a Paradise police cruiser was parked in front of her house, and Jesse Stone leaning against it.

"What are you doing here," she said.

"Waiting for you," he said.

"Waiting for me why?"

"I wanted to talk with you."

"What about?"

"Mr. Tauber."

"Mr. Tauber my homeroom teacher?"

"None other."

"What about Mr. Tauber?"

"Do you like him?"

"Not much."

"Is he a good teacher?"

"I only have him for homeroom."

"Is he a good homeroom teacher?"

"He doesn't really teach in homeroom," Julie said.

"What does he do there?"

"During school he mostly checks attendance and makes announcements. Stuff like that."

"And after school?"

"He supervises detention."

"Detention as in staying after school?"

"Yes."

"Have you ever had detention?"

"You're kidding, right?"

"Have you ever had it?"

"Of course I've had it."

"Because?"

"They say I have attitude issues," Julie said.

"I can't imagine why."

"Was that meant as a put-down, Chief Stone?"

"Jesse."

"You want me to call you Jesse?"

"It's my name."

"Okay, Jesse," Julie said, after a moment. "Was that a put-down?"

"An observation."

Julie didn't say anything.

"What does one do in detention," Jesse said.

"Mostly homework. Except if you're willing to please Mr. Tauber. Then you get to go home early."

"What does that mean?"

"I don't want to talk about it."

"You don't want to talk about what it means to please Mr. Tauber."

"No."

"Why?"

Julie didn't say anything.

"Does this embarrass you for some reason," Jesse said.

"It might."

"And you don't want to tell me why?"

"No."

"Have you ever told anyone?"

"No."

"Would it help if you told someone," Jesse said.

"It would make things worse."

"Because?"

"Because he told us it would."

"Mr. Tauber said that if you told anyone about pleasing him, it would make things worse for you?"

"Yes."

"In what way?"

"Our grades would be lowered. We would get into trouble with the other teachers."

"So Mr. Tauber threatened you?"

"Yes."

"What did he do to you, Julie?"

Julie didn't say anything.

"He obviously did something which he knew would reflect badly on him. What did he do, Julie?"

After several moments she said, "He made us sit on his lap."

"And what did he do when you sat on his lap," Jesse said.

"You know, stuff."

"What kind of stuff?"

"He would touch me."

"Touch you."

"He liked to touch my boobies."

"Mr. Tauber touched your breasts?"

"Yes."

"Did he do the same with any of the other girls," Jesse said.

"I think so."

"Who else?"

"Maybe Lesly and Bonnie."

"Did they tell anyone?"

"No."

"Because he instructed them not to?"

"I guess."

"There are consequences for that kind of behavior," Jesse said.

"Which means?"

"Let's just say that I don't think he'll be doing it again."

"Who's gonna stop him?"

"I am."

They were quiet.

"Was that all you wanted," Julie said.

"Lisa Barry," Jesse said.

"What about her?"

"Will you speak to a therapist?"

"The shrink?"

"Yes."

"Maybe. If you make me."

"You're a smart girl, Julie. One day you'll be a smart woman. This could be a defining moment for you," Jesse said.

"What's that supposed to mean?"

"What you did to Lisa Barry was cruel and hurtful. As you grow up and you reflect on your actions, which you will, you'll be ashamed of them. It will gnaw at you."

Julie didn't say anything.

"Talk to a therapist. He or she can help you understand the real cause of what you did."

"I don't know about seeing a shrink."

After a moment, Jesse said, "I see a shrink."

"You?"

"Me."

"Wow."

"I like to think of it as a learning experience. Just like a class. Only this class is one where you learn about yourself."

"So it's a good thing?"

"If you meet it head-on, it could be one of the best things you'll ever do."

"You're a strange guy."

"Me?"

"Talking to me like this."

"Like how?"

"Like I'm a grown-up."

"In many cultures you would not only be regarded a grown-up, but you'd probably already be married."

"Really?"

"You could look it up."

"I like you, Chief Stone."

"Jesse," he said.

"Jesse," she said.

"I like you, too, Julie."

49

"So forensics confirmed he was dead before the explosion," Healy said.

"Yes," Jesse said.

Jesse was in his office, drinking coffee, speaking with Healy on the phone.

"What did you make of that," Healy said.

"I had an epiphany," Jesse said.

"Meaning?"

"A sudden realization."

"I wasn't asking for the definition of the word," Healy said.

"With you, one never knows."

"What was your epiphany?"

"Rollo Nurse," Jesse said.

"Who's Rollo Nurse?"

"The ex-con who Captain Cronjager thought might be coming for me."

Healy didn't say anything.

"I believe he's here."

"In Paradise?"

"Yes."

"So what are you going to do?"

"I'm gonna find him. I'm gonna step up the night patrols. Check all the motels and residential hotels. Ask around town about him."

"A start," Healy said.

"A start," Jesse said.

"You'll be on alert?"

"I'm always on alert," Jesse said.

"Except when you're not," Healy said.

Jesse gave instructions to Perkins, Suitcase, and Bauer to increase the number of cars on night patrol from two to eight. He ordered two officers per vehicle. No more solo patrols.

He distributed copies of the photo taken of Rollo Nurse at his release from Lompoc State Prison. It had been faxed by Captain Cronjager at Jesse's request. He ordered that these photos be shown at every residence facility that might cater to transients, as well as convenience stores and liquor shops.

He made certain everyone knew that Rollo Nurse was to be considered armed and dangerous. Appropriate caution should be exercised in any potential exchange with him.

Jesse let them know he would also be part

of the night-patrol team.

Stuart Tauber pulled his late-model Taurus into the driveway of his house. He got out and was heading for the front door when he spotted Jesse, across the street, leaning against his cruiser. Tauber walked cautiously toward him.

"You again," he said.

"Yep," Jesse said.

Tauber crossed the street and approached him.

"What do you want this time," he said.

"I wanted to see where you live."

"You've seen it. Now you can leave."

"Do you have kids, Mr. Tauber?"

"That would be none of your business."

"Records say you have a son."

"If you already knew, why did you ask?"

"Is your son in any danger?"

"What's that supposed to mean?"

"Do you abuse your son, Mr. Tauber?"

"What kind of question is that?"

"Do you restrict your activities only to young girls, or are you an equal-opportunity abuser?"

"I've had quite enough of you, Stone."

"Does your wife know," Jesse said.

"I'm calling my lawyer," Tauber said.

"Good idea."

"What?"

"You're going to need a lawyer, Tauber," Jesse said.

Tauber glared at him.

Then he turned, crossed the street, and went inside his house.

Jesse brought his findings to Assistant District Attorney Martin Reagan.

"What do you want to do about this," Reagan said.

"I want to arrest him. Make a spectacle of it. In front of the entire school."

"How will you do that?"

"At the Friday-morning assembly."

"Are you sure the girls will testify?"

"One of them surely will. The others will follow," Jesse said.

"I'll prepare the paperwork."

"Try not to hurt yourself."

"Not to worry. That's why the government provides us with assistants."

"I knew there was a reason."

When Jesse finally got home, he poured himself a scotch. He was unnerved by Rollo Nurse. He had remembered the night when he thought he heard strange noises. Maybe it had been Rollo. Maybe he knew where Jesse lived.

He took his scotch upstairs and was surprised to find Mildred Memory asleep on his bed. She had been spending more and more time indoors. She was becoming domesticated.

When Jesse tried to get into bed, he encountered a problem. Mildred Memory was stretched out diagonally across the bed, which left very little room for him. He attempted to push her out of his way, but that made her all the more resolute. Finally, he picked her up, got himself comfortable, and then placed her back down. She looked at him with half-closed eyes, then stretched out again, making it eminently clear she regarded the bed as hers.

Jesse smiled.

Working around the cat, he made himself as comfortable as he could, then went to sleep.

50

On Friday morning, Jesse and Suitcase were standing at the rear of the junior high school auditorium, awaiting the start of the weekly assembly. A number of the students had noticed the two officers, and the crowd was starting to buzz.

The assembly came to order. The pledge of allegiance was recited. Eleanor Nelson took the podium. She was just beginning her opening remarks when Jesse and Suitcase made their move.

They spotted Tauber and walked toward him. A hush came over the auditorium. Mrs. Nelson stopped speaking.

"Stuart Tauber," Jesse said.

Mr. Tauber looked at Jesse with alarm.

"Yes," he said.

"You are under arrest for the crime of sexual abuse of a minor. Officer Simpson will read you your rights."

A collective gasp could be heard in the

auditorium.

Mrs. Nelson stared unblinkingly at the unfolding scenario.

Suitcase began to read Tauber his rights.

Jesse looked around. He spotted Lisa Barry, with whom he made eye contact. He saw Julie Knoller, who was smiling.

When Suitcase finished, he took a pair of handcuffs from his service belt. Holding Tauber's hands behind his back, he cuffed him.

Then Jesse yanked Mr. Tauber out of his row and began walking him up the aisle. Tauber's head was lowered. His eyes were on the floor.

A cry of "Boo, Tauber" began to arise. It grew louder as more of the audience became emboldened.

Julie Knoller stood and began to applaud rhythmically. Before long, many of the students joined her.

As Jesse led Mr. Tauber out of the auditorium, the boos and the rhythmic applause had become deafening.

Jesse pulled his cruiser to a stop in front of Hathaway's Previously Owned Quality Vehicles. He went inside.

Hasty was in his office. The door was open. Jesse knocked.

"It's open," Hasty said.

Jesse entered.

"Are you here to arrest me," Hasty said.

"I bet you say that to all the cops."

"How did you know?"

"I want you to do something for me," Jesse said, as he sat down in front of Hasty's desk.

"What do you want," Hasty said.

"I want you to pretend that I'm a car salesman."

"What?"

"I want to sell you a couple of used Hondas."

Hasty snorted.

"You can't be serious," he said.

"I couldn't be more serious," Jesse said.

"I'm not interested," Hasty said.

"I'll offer you an excellent deal."

"I'm still not interested."

"Hasty, I want you to open your mind to the advantages of making this deal with me."

"There are no advantages."

"You're wrong about that. The big advantage is that by buying these Hondas, you'll be performing your civic duty," Jesse said.

"Something tells me that these are the same two Hondas which I sold to you. Correct?"

"Correct."

"And you want me to buy them back from you."

"Correct again."

Hasty didn't say anything.

"Say yes, Hasty."

"No."

"I'd consider it a personal favor."

"No. How much do you want for them?"

"Same as I paid."

"The same as you paid," Hasty said.

"Yes."

"No."

"Come on, Hasty. You know you're gonna do it."

"This is highway robbery."

"It's for the good of Paradise."

"Why do you want to sell them?"

"I'm done with them."

"What about the car thefts?"

"Finished."

"How do you know?"

"I'm the police chief. I know everything."

"What you paid less twenty percent," Hasty said.

"No."

"Fifteen percent."

"This isn't a negotiation, Hasty."

"You have to let me make something on the deal," Hasty said.

"No, I don't," Jesse said.

238

"Why are you being such a hard-ass," Hasty said.

"Because Paradise needs the money."

Hasty didn't say anything.

"So it's a deal?"

"I didn't say that."

"You implied it, though."

"I did not."

"The check goes to Carter Hansen," Jesse said.

"You can't imagine how much this hurts me," Hasty said.

"Cut the crap, Hasty. You'll be bragging about this within the hour."

"Where are the vehicles?"

"They'll be here momentarily," Jesse said.

"Don't go thinking this means you own me," Hasty said.

"How could you say such a thing," Jesse said.

51

Jesse fed Mildred Memory and left the house to join the night-patrol team. Thus far the search had turned up nothing. No one recognized the photo of Rollo Nurse. No one remembered having seen him. The stepped-up night patrol had garnered no results. He was prepared for a long night.

Several minutes after Jesse left, Rollo emerged from the darkness at the entrance to the footbridge. He walked swiftly across it.

He went around to the porch doors, and after determining they were locked, he smashed a glass pane on one of them.

He reached inside, mindful of the broken glass. He turned the knob and opened the door.

He went inside.

So this is how he lives, thought Rollo, as he looked around the house. *Not so fancy. His things aren't so fancy.*

He took out his flashlight and his bowie knife. He began to systematically destroy the living room. He smashed lamps. He slammed the TV to the floor. He broke glasses. He sliced open the leather armchairs and ripped out the stuffing. He upended the desk.

In the kitchen, he noticed the bowls of food that had been placed on the floor. He picked one of them up and caught a whiff of cat food.

He continued his destruction.

But now he was also searching for a cat.

Suitcase drove and Jesse rode shotgun as they joined the night patrol. There was no sign of Rollo.

Somewhere between three and four a.m., they decided to call it a night. Suitcase was hungry, and he convinced Jesse to accompany him to a highway diner.

Suitcase ordered the breakfast special. Three eggs with sausage and home fries. He slathered his sourdough toast with butter and jelly, and washed it down with a super-sized Diet Coke.

Jesse had coffee.

"I didn't think I'd be eating alone," Suitcase said.

"But you compensated by eating enough

for us both," Jesse said.

"I'm still growing," Suitcase said.

"Yes, but in which direction," Jesse said.

Jesse noticed that the waitress, a pretty woman named Debby, was particularly solicitous of Suitcase's dining needs. She hovered over him when she took his order. She brushed up against him when she served it. She kept returning to ask if everything was all right.

He also noticed that Suitcase interrupted his gourmandizing to watch Debby every time she sauntered by.

"You got something going with her," Jesse said.

"What do you mean," Suitcase said.

"Debby. The waitress. You got something going with her?"

"Why do you ask?"

"Come on, Suit. The only thing that tears your attention away from your food is the sight of her ass."

"That's not a nice thing to say, Jesse."

"But it's true."

Suitcase didn't say anything.

"So," Jesse said.

"Maybe."

"What maybe?"

"We went to high school together," Suitcase said.

"And?"

"We dated."

"And?"

"She wanted to get married, and I didn't."

Jesse didn't say anything.

"So she married someone else."

"And?"

"Stop saying 'and.' "

Jesse shrugged.

"So she got married to someone else," Jesse said.

"Yes," Suitcase said.

"And?"

"She got divorced."

"Kids?"

"Two."

Jesse didn't say anything.

"We fool around," Suitcase said.

"Serious?"

"Not serious. She's got two kids, for God's sake."

"But you like each other."

"After a fashion."

"What's that supposed to mean?"

"We like each other, but we're not serious," Suitcase said.

"Is she the reason we came here?"

"It's a toss-up."

"A toss-up?"

"The breakfast special was a big attraction."

"And Debby?"

"She was a big attraction, too."

"Which isn't obvious in any way."

"Is it obvious," Suitcase said.

"Do firemen wear red suspenders," Jesse said.

Jesse knew something was wrong as soon as he crossed the footbridge. He could sense it. He unholstered his pistol, turned on his high-beam flashlight, and began to circle the house. He saw that the front door was off its hinges, hanging open. He noticed the damaged porch doors. He went inside.

The devastation was total. Everything that could possibly have been broken, was. He stepped over shattered glass and overturned furniture. Nothing was as it had been.

He stepped onto the patio. The love seat had been cut open and its innards strewn about.

He went upstairs and found the remains of his bedroom. The mattress had been slashed. The furniture lay splintered on the floor.

He called for Mildred Memory, but she didn't appear, which alarmed him. He righted one of his kitchen chairs and sat down heavily, his head in his hands.

He knew it was Rollo Nurse.

He phoned Molly. Dawn was just breaking. She told him she'd be right over.

After having examined the wreckage, Molly sat down alongside Jesse.

"We can fix this," she said.

He shrugged.

"You're worried about the cat," she said.

"I am."

"She'll turn up. Cats have a way of doing that."

He didn't say anything.

Because Jesse's phone had been ripped from the wall, Molly used her cell to make several calls. One was to Captain Healy.

Healy stopped by on his way to Boston.

"Rollo Nurse," he said.

"Be my guess," Jesse said.

"He's getting bolder," Healy said.

"He is," Jesse said.

"What's next?"

"I have to find him."

"He could be anywhere."

"He could."

Healy didn't say anything.

"I'm going to put more boots on the ground. Ratchet up the surveillance. He's bound to slip up," Jesse said.

"He hasn't yet."

The two men didn't speak for a while.

Then Jesse said, "Mildred Memory is missing."

"She's missing?"

"I haven't found her."

Healy considered this for a while.

"Have you looked under the furniture," he said.

"Under what furniture? It's all ruined."

Healy went onto the porch. Although the love seat had been decimated, it still stood upright. He knelt down and looked beneath it.

"Come here, Jesse," he said.

Jesse stepped outside.

"Look under the love seat," Healy said.

Jesse knelt down and looked.

The first thing he saw were the eyes. They squarely met his gaze. When he reached for her, the cat began to inch its way from her cramped hiding place. When she emerged, Jesse picked her up and held her.

"How did you know," Jesse said.

"Cat Whisperer," Healy said.

52

Jesse left Molly to look after the house and drove to the station. Suitcase was waiting for him when he pulled his cruiser into his parking spot.

"I'm sorry about your house, Jesse," Suitcase said.

"At least it's still standing," Jesse said.

"There's that," Suitcase said.

When they went inside, Jesse found three visitors waiting to see him. One was Eleanor Nelson, the junior high school principal. There was an older woman whom he didn't recognize. The third was Robert Lopresti.

He acknowledged them all, then went to his office. Suit brought him some fresh coffee.

"I'll see them one by one," Jesse said. "Ask Mrs. Nelson to step in, and let the other two know I'll be with them shortly. Thanks for the coffee."

"Are you as tired as me," Suit said.

"At the very least," Jesse said.

"I made the coffee strong."

"Maybe there's a God after all," Jesse said.

Suitcase smiled.

"How'd things go with Debby," Jesse said.

"Why do you think I'm so tired?"

"I'm sorry I asked."

"What do you think Lopresti wants," Suitcase said.

"Beats me," Jesse said. "Took balls for him to show up, though. Tell him I'll see him as soon as I can. Who's the old lady?"

"Don't know. She said she needed to speak directly to you."

Jesse sighed.

Suitcase left, and Mrs. Nelson came in.

"Thank you for seeing me, Chief Stone."

"Sit down, please," Jesse said.

She did.

"I wanted you to know that I've decided to resign my position."

Jesse didn't say anything.

"At the end of the day," Mrs. Nelson said, "I believe you were right. I've been negligent in the performance of my duties."

Jesse remained silent.

"I became aware of that fact when you arrested Mr. Tauber. I should have known about him, but somehow . . ." Mrs. Nelson said.

Jesse still didn't say anything.

"I'm not trying to make excuses for myself. Upon reflection, I came to realize that over time my job had become different. With the economy faltering, my attentions were more focused on administrative concerns. Layoffs. Reductions in services. Making do with less. The demands of the job increased. Conditions changed. I changed. As a result, I lost sight of the very thing that should have been paramount, as you so aptly put it. I'm horrified that I wasn't aware of what Tauber had been doing. I'm embarrassed by how badly I mishandled Lisa Barry."

Jesse remained silent.

"The rules regarding bullying are so vague," she said. "Did the incident occur on campus or off? Was it in-person bullying, or was it the cyberspace kind? Was it physical or psychological? I guess I'm guilty of having buried my head in the sand."

"Why are you telling me this?"

"Because you helped open my eyes."

"Have you discussed this with the members of the school board?"

"No."

"Have you submitted your resignation," Jesse said.

"I sent them a letter."

"To which they replied?"

"They haven't yet."

"Perhaps you should request a meeting. To at least inform them of what you've told me. To make them aware of the changes which affected your job performance so dramatically."

"What difference would that make," Mrs. Nelson said.

"A big one. You could explain to them how things evolved and discuss ways in which they might be bettered," Jesse said.

"Knowing what you think of me, why would you make such a suggestion?"

"Because of what you just told me."

"Meaning?"

"I understand your situation more clearly."

"What about separating me from my job, as you so eloquently put it?"

"People are allowed to change their minds."

"Are you suggesting that you changed your mind, Chief Stone?"

"Jesse," Jesse said.

"Jesse," Mrs. Nelson said.

"I am, Mrs. Nelson."

"Eleanor," she said.

"Eleanor."

Mrs. Nelson had to look away for a moment.

"Thank you, Jesse," Mrs. Nelson said. "I believe I can convince the board to allow me to rescind my resignation and discuss these issues with me. I think I can help effectuate change."

"Change would be good," Jesse said.

She stood.

He stood.

She reached out her hand. He took it.

"Let me know if there's anything I can do to help," he said.

"I will," she said.

After Mrs. Nelson left, Jesse asked Suitcase to bring in Robert Lopresti.

"This is a surprise," said Jesse, when Lopresti entered his office.

"I hope you're not gonna kill me," Robert said.

"Not just yet," Jesse said. "Why are you here?"

"You're the only one I can talk to," Lopresti said.

"About what," Jesse said.

"You were honorable with me," Lopresti said. "You lived up to your word."

Jesse didn't say anything.

"I guess you heard that Mr. Lombardo got aced," Lopresti said.

"Eloquently stated."

"When I was in that room, I had the

chance to do some thinking. You told me that I was one of the bad guys. I never thought of myself like that before. I got kids, you know. They missed me. My wife was never so scared as when I was being held. I got to thinking that I'd like to stop being a bad guy."

"And you're telling me this because . . . ?"

"Because I want you to help me."

"You want me to help you," Jesse said.

"Yeah."

"Help you how?"

"I want to get a job in Paradise."

"A job?"

"Yeah."

"What kind of job?"

"I'm a great mechanic," Robert said. "Always have been. I just never did it legitimately."

"Define 'great mechanic.' "

"There's nothing I don't know about cars. I can take 'em apart and rebuild 'em. I know every part of every car. Cars are in my blood."

"And you want me to find you a job as a mechanic," Jesse said.

"Yeah."

"So that you can think of yourself as a good guy?"

"So my family can be proud of me."

Jesse didn't say anything.

"My wife and my kids," Robert said.

Jesse thought for a while.

"Let Officer Simpson know how I can reach you."

"You think you can help?"

"Maybe."

"I was hopin' you would. That would be so great. Thanks, Chief Stone."

"Jesse."

"Yeah."

When Lopresti left, Jesse asked Suitcase for more coffee. Then he told him to bring in the old lady.

"My name is Agatha Miller," she said, as she sat down.

"Mrs. Miller," Jesse said.

"Miss Miller," she said.

"Okay," Jesse said. "What can I do for you, Miss Miller?"

"It's about my boarder."

"Your boarder?"

"Yes," she said. "Donald Johnson."

"What about Donald Johnson," Jesse said.

"He's strange," she said.

"In what way?"

"He never goes out during the day. He only goes at night."

"At night?"

"Yes. When he thinks I'm asleep, he goes out the back door."

Jesse leaned toward Miss Miller.

"How long has he been boarding with you, Miss Miller?"

"Nearly a month," she said. "He told me he was here for vacation. He's from Kansas."

"Would you be able to identify him from a photograph," Jesse said.

"Perhaps," she said. "My eyes aren't what they used to be, though."

Jesse asked Suitcase to bring in the photo of Rollo Nurse. He handed it to Miss Miller, who looked at it closely. First she looked at it with her heavy-duty glasses on, then with them off.

"Is this man Donald Johnson," Jesse said.

"I think so," she said. "Yes. I think so."

53

As soon as Agatha Miller left the house, Rollo sensed that something was wrong. The voices were raised. They had become insistent.

He packed his belongings and slipped out of the house.

He left the neighborhood and quickly walked to the nearby park. Certain no one had noticed him, he disappeared into the brush and settled down to wait for dark.

Some weeks earlier he had made a safe place for himself in the deep woods on the outskirts of town. He had dug out a small area in a bushy glen. He purchased some used camping gear, gathered a few supplies, and stowed them all in the clearing. Once darkness descended, he would leave the park and head there. He would hide out and wait for the appropriate time to make his final move on Jesse Stone.

He throbbed with excitement. It had all

gone so smoothly. The voices hadn't led him astray. Soon he would swoop down and destroy Jesse Stone, just as Jesse Stone had destroyed him. In the end, he would still be alive. And Jesse Stone wouldn't.

Jesse followed Agatha Miller to her home. He was accompanied by Suitcase and Perkins.

She ushered Jesse and Suitcase inside. Then she pointed Perkins to the back of the house. All three officers had their weapons drawn.

Miss Miller showed Jesse and Suitcase to Rollo's room, then she left the house at Jesse's instruction.

Jesse took up a position alongside the door to Rollo's room. Suitcase was behind him in the kitchen.

"Rollo, this is Jesse Stone," he said. "Open the door and come out with your hands above your head."

There was no response.

Jesse repeated the instruction.

Still no response.

He tried the handle of the door. It was unlocked. He pushed the door open and dove inside. He hit the floor and rolled to a sitting position, his pistol in his hand.

The room was empty.

Jesse checked the bathroom. It, too, was empty. He called to both Suitcase and Perkins.

They carefully searched the room, but Rollo had stripped it of his personal effects. All he left behind was the photo of himself that had been circulated around town, a copy of which he had placed on the night table.

The three officers looked at one another.

"What's next," Suitcase said.

"Beats me," Jesse said.

Jesse called Gino from his cell phone.

"Jesse Stone," Gino said, when he picked up the call. "As we say in gangland, how may I help you?"

"Gangland?"

"A euphemism."

"Do you offer a retirement policy," Jesse said.

"Excuse me?"

"You know, a policy that allows gangland members to hang them up, so to speak."

"I'm not certain I'm following you, Jesse Stone," Gino said.

"Let's say there was someone who worked on the technical side of things, who wanted to take the opportunity of his benefactor's recent demise to quit the business. Get out of the game."

"I'm listening," Gino said.

"Might there be unfortunate consequences as a result of such an action?"

"How about we get to the point," Gino said. "What exactly do you want to know?"

"Would you or any of your associates come after such a person, were he to voluntarily retire," Jesse said.

"Would he involve himself with a competing organization?"

"No. He would be going legit."

"What's your interest in the matter," Gino said.

"I was approached by this young man, who claims to have developed concerns both for his own safety and for the safety of his family."

"And you're inquiring on his behalf?"

"I am."

Gino was quiet.

"I can't foresee any potential health problems for your friend. So long as he doesn't cross paths with any of the company's interests."

"He won't."

"How do you know he won't?"

"Trust me, I know."

"Trust you?"

"A euphemism."

"Do I get to know your friend's name?"

"Robert Lopresti."

"I kind of figured," Gino said.

"I kind of figured you'd kind of figure," Jesse said.

"Please send my good wishes to Mr. Lopresti."

"I shall."

"And my altogether best wishes to you, Jesse Stone," Gino said.

"I kind of figured that, too," Jesse said.

54

Although Jesse ordered a neighborhood dragnet, it turned up no sign of Rollo Nurse. He seemed to have vanished. No animal killings were reported. There were no more fires. Outwardly, Paradise regained its sense of normalcy. The police department, however, was on the highest level of alert.

Jesse returned home, weary, prepared to spend the next several days restoring the contents of his house. When he parked at the entrance to the footbridge, he discovered the Striar Brothers delivery van. The driver and his assistant were just leaving.

"The bed's as good as new, Jesse," the driver said. Jesse looked at him.

"Mr. Striar made certain we got it on the truck today."

The two men waved to Jesse as they pulled away.

Jesse crossed the footbridge and went

inside. He was astonished by what he saw.

The house had been completely restored. The broken, vandalized pieces were gone. New furniture had replaced the old.

In the center of the refurbished living room stood Molly, with an enormous grin on her face.

Jesse stared at her.

"I'll be expecting something extra in my paycheck," she said.

Jesse was quiet.

"I don't provide this kind of service to just any bozo, you know," she said.

Jesse still didn't say anything.

"Shame you can't be silent more often," Molly said.

"This is incredible."

"You have a lot of friends in this town, Jesse."

"But . . ."

"I wish I had videotaped what went on here today."

"Do you want to tell me about it," he said.

"Can I use big words?"

Jesse didn't say anything.

"Rennie's Cleaning was here first. They salvaged what they could and carted off the rest. The merchants tripped all over themselves in an effort to replace what had been destroyed. There were so many trucks, the drivers were forced to line up and wait their turn for delivery."

"How can I afford this," he said.

"You won't have to," she said.

"Excuse me?"

"The items were all deeply discounted. Tokens of how much people around here appreciate you, Jesse. Don't ask me why."

"I can't accept them. I can't take gifts," he said.

"Board of selectmen paid for them."

"What?"

"The board of selectmen went into emergency session, and after consulting with each merchant, they agreed to create a special fund to pay for it all. It was a unanimous vote, by the way."

Jesse didn't say anything.

He looked around. There was a new love seat on the porch, new leather armchairs in the living room. A new TV. New dishware and glasses were in the kitchen, along with a new table, new chairs, and a new refrigerator.

Upstairs there was a new bed, new mattress, and new linens. The bedside tables and the bureau had been repaired.

Asleep on the bed was Mildred Memory.

"I'm gonna go home now," Molly said.

"What can I say," Jesse said.

"There aren't words enough to thank me."

"I'm speechless," Jesse said.

"Take two aspirin and call me in the morning," Molly said, as she went downstairs.

Jesse followed.

She gathered her things and headed for the newly repaired door. She turned to find Jesse standing next to her. He hugged her.

"Arghhh," she said. "Don't go getting all gooey on me, Jesse."

She smiled to herself as she walked away from the house.

55

Following an uneventful night, one in which a patrol car was a constant presence at the entrance to the footbridge, Jesse made a stop at the Town Hall.

He found Carter Hansen at his desk.

"May I come in," Jesse said.

"I have no way of stopping you," Hansen said.

"Thank you, Carter," Jesse said.

"No thanks are necessary," Hansen said.

"I'm grateful nonetheless."

"People here like you, Jesse," Hansen said. "The outpouring of generosity is testament to that."

"I'm speechless," Jesse said.

"Then I'll understand when you don't say good-bye," Hansen said.

Jesse smiled.

Rather than leave the building, however, he stopped by Alexis Richardson's office and stuck his head in.

"I heard," Alexis said, motioning for him to come in.

"An unusual series of events," Jesse said.

"Try not to overreact," Alexis said.

"I had a thought, in case you're interested," Jesse said.

"And you wish to share it?"

"Only if you're interested."

"Okay. I'm interested."

"Will there be any acoustic acts?"

"I'm sorry?"

"Acoustic acts? Softer music," Jesse said.

"Why do you ask?"

"It's not polite to answer a question with another question," Jesse said.

"I didn't realize you placed such stock in grammatical formalities."

"We're drifting off point," Jesse said.

"Yes," she said.

"Yes what?"

"Yes, there will be acoustic acts. Why?"

"If you were to schedule those acts for the end of the concert, and as a result, greatly reduce the levels of the amplification system, you might just have a viable argument for a time extension."

"You mean if the speaker system was turned way down, we could play past eleven o'clock?"

"It's possible."

"How?"

"Because the eleven o'clock curfew rule was put in place so that the neighborhood would be spared the discomfort of loudly amplified music."

"And if the music was minimally amplified, we could play it beyond the curfew."

"It would need to be closely monitored, of course. The noise levels in the adjoining neighborhoods would have to be negligible."

"And who would do the monitoring?"

"The police department."

"And you thought of this?"

"An epiphany."

"Why?"

"Because I'm the police chief. I take everyone's interests into consideration."

"Even mine?"

"Even yours."

Alexis looked at him.

"Thank you, Jesse," she said.

"All in a day's work," he said.

56

"So then what happened," Jesse said.

"She actually said hello to me," Lisa Barry said.

They were strolling in Paradise Park, where Jesse had brought her after picking her up at school.

"Did she say anything else?"

"She acted kind of sheepish," Lisa said. "She walked a ways with me and tried to be friendly."

"Julie's a complicated young woman," Jesse said.

"What's that supposed to mean?"

"It means that although she's a person of privilege, she still harbors a great deal of anger. She acts on instinct, without really understanding why."

"That sounds like shrink talk."

"It is shrink talk."

"You place a lot of stock in analysis, don't you, Jesse?"

"If gone about correctly, it can be an invaluable tool for self-realization."

"Which means?"

"Analysis can provide the foundation for a healthy life," Jesse said.

"Is that why you think my speaking with Dr. Canter is so important?"

"Yes."

"Well, I am speaking with her."

"And?"

"I like it."

"Because?"

"Because we talk about things which I wouldn't talk about otherwise."

"Which is a good thing?"

"Yes."

"And school?"

"Everyone's still talking about how you arrested Mr. Tauber."

"He deserved to be arrested."

After a while Lisa said, "Mrs. Nelson came to see me."

Jesse didn't say anything.

"She said she was sorry for what she did. She forgave me for holding her. She said I should come to her if I ever have issues."

"How did you feel about that?"

"I felt good. She was different. She seemed genuine," Lisa said.

"Sometimes people lose sight of right and wrong."

"You think Mrs. Nelson lost sight of right and wrong?"

"I do. But when she realized that she had, she took steps to rectify it. She deserves credit for that," Jesse said.

"Is that why you're not mad at her anymore?"

"Yes."

"Do you know the difference between right and wrong, Jesse?"

"I try to know it, Lisa."

"And sometimes you don't?"

"Nobody's perfect," Jesse said.

They walked in silence for a while.

Rollo Nurse stepped cautiously from his sanctuary in the woods. It was late afternoon, and he was restless. He was anxious to finish the job.

He could see it all in his mind. He could visualize everything the voices had instructed. He hadn't experienced such clearheadedness in ages. He felt strong. Like the old Rollo. Things were going his way.

But it was too early, he determined. Darkness was still some time away. The last thing he wanted was to be seen in daylight. His picture was everywhere. People would recognize him.

He slipped back into the glade. He would wait. He had come this far.

On his way back to the station, Jesse stopped off at Hathaway's Previously Owned Quality Vehicles. He knocked on Hasty's door, which was open.

"It's open," he said.

Jesse went inside.

"You're too late, Officer," Hasty said. "I'm already lawyered up."

"Are you feeling civic-minded, Hasty," Jesse said, as he sat down.

"I'm always feeling civic-minded," Hasty said.

"Are you a forgiving person," Jesse said.

"Cut the crap, Jesse. What do you want?"

"I want you to give someone a job."

"Who? What kind of job?"

"A former mobster."

"You want me to give a job to a former mobster? What are you, crazy?"

"You're a former mobster," Jesse said.

"I am not. At least not technically. Assisting a mobster and actually being one are two different things," Hasty said.

"Nitpicking," Jesse said.

"Who is this former mobster?"

"One of John Lombardo's chop-shop mechanics."

"A mechanic?"

"A very good mechanic."

"Why do you want me to hire this mechanic?"

"Because I believe he's seeking legitimacy," Jesse said.

"Why?"

"So he can feel good about his life."

At first Hasty didn't say anything.

"That's why you want me to hire him," he said.

"Also because, as an ex-convict, you can be a role model for him."

"I'm not a good role model for anyone," Hasty said.

"Don't be so sure, Hasty. You've done a very impressive job of resurrecting your life and your career."

"My wife still won't talk to me."

"Ex-wife, Hasty. You need to get past that. Redemption, remember?"

"I know. I know," Hasty said. "Maybe I could use a good mechanic."

"Will you talk to him?"

"What's his name?"

"Robert Lopresti. Can I have him call you?"

"Okay. All right."

"Thank you, Hasty." Jesse stood up. "And

thank you for what you did on the board."

"No thanks necessary."

"But tendered just the same."

57

Jesse rode around town for a while. He wrote a few parking tickets. He took a moment to catch his breath.

He was certain that the Rollo Nurse scenario was heading toward the finish line. Although he had managed to elude capture so far, Rollo had been flushed from his hideout and was essentially on the run. People were looking for him. He wouldn't go unnoticed much longer.

Jesse was certain that he was the final target. Even though there was now twenty-four-hour surveillance on his house, he wasn't taking Rollo for granted. He knew he was vulnerable.

He was satisfied that the car theft adventure was finished and had cost a dangerous criminal his life. He still remembered the look in Nancy Lytell's eyes. He took some small measure of satisfaction at having avenged her husband's killing.

Assistant DA Marty Reagan was about to indict Mr. Tauber, who would be facing some serious jail time. Jesse was certain that further investigation would reveal other incidents of abuse. He fully expected more youngsters to come forward. Men like Tauber were toxic.

He'd relished the look in Alexis Richardson's eyes when he had suggested a way out of her dilemma. He liked her. He admired her resolute manner. He wished her success.

He wrote a few more tickets, then went to the station.

Molly was there to greet him.

"Can I get you some coffee," she said.

"What's wrong," Jesse said.

"Wrong?"

"Why would you offer to get me coffee?"

"I don't know. What difference does it make?"

"A big one. You have frequently used coffee as a tool to bust my chops."

"You noticed?"

"I did."

"Well, maybe today is an off day."

"An off day?"

"The once-a-year 'don't bust Jesse's chops' day," Molly said.

Jesse didn't say anything.

"You should be grateful," she said.

Jesse watched her leave.

He phoned Robert Lopresti.

"Have you got a pencil handy," he said, when Robert answered.

"Jesse?"

"Yep."

"I just got one."

"Paper?"

"That, too."

Jesse gave him Hasty's number.

"When you meet with him, try to be impressive," Jesse said.

"I'm always impressive," Robert said.

"Not that anyone would notice."

"You noticed."

Jesse didn't say anything.

"Enough to put me up for the job."

"I hope you get it, Robert."

"I'll let you know."

"Please do."

"Thanks for this, Jesse."

"Don't mention it."

58

The first thing Rollo saw was the patrol car with two officers inside. It was parked near the entrance to the footbridge, which made it impossible for him to gain easy access to Jesse's house.

The only way to bypass the car unnoticed was to swim. He thought about that for a while. He had his shoulder bag with him, in which he had placed several cans of lighter fluid. He was carrying a throwaway lighter in his pocket. He would have to keep them dry. His duffel wasn't waterproof, and he hadn't thought to bring any plastic bags.

He could attack the occupants of the patrol car, but he didn't like his odds. He decided to swim.

He walked away from the footbridge, crossed a rocky promontory, and made his way to the water's edge, which was out of sight of the patrol car. Once there, he took off his clothes, folded them and placed them inside the duffel. He would try to hug the shoreline as much as possible, holding the bag high above his head in order to prevent it from getting wet.

He entered the water. It was startlingly cold.

The floor of the bay was rocky. There was very little sand. Walking was difficult. He submerged and, holding the duffel above the water, he started to paddle.

He made his way into deeper water. The cold rattled his bones. He swam as best he could while holding the bag out of the water. The going was slow, but he made steady progress, and he soon rounded the curve in the shoreline and was approaching the far side of the house.

He inched his way to the water's edge and, stepping over the stones, came ashore.

He was frozen. He shook the water off as best he could. He had no towel. He put his clothes on. They absorbed the wet but didn't dry him. Cold and miserable, he headed for the back of the house. The only consolation for his discomfort was the knowledge that he would soon be triumphant.

Jesse lay down on the bed and turned on the old-movie channel. He had grown to like the oldies better than the new ones. He was settling in to watch Henry Fonda and Barbara Stanwyck in the Preston Sturges classic *The Lady Eve* when he heard a loud knocking on his door.

Has to be one of the patrol-car cops wanting to use the bathroom, he surmised.

He put the TV on mute and went downstairs. He stopped in the kitchen to grab his Colt and walked to the door.

When he opened it, he discovered Alexis Richardson standing there. She looked at him demurely and held up a sack of Chinese takeout.

"Déjà vu all over again," Jesse said.

"You gonna invite me in," Alexis said.

"I'm thinking about it," he said.

"What's with the gun," she said.

"I'm a cop," Jesse said.

She looked at him.

Then he stepped aside, and she swept past him into the house. He accompanied her to the kitchen, where he took the food from her and placed it on the counter, along with his Colt.

"To what do I owe the honor," he said.

"I wanted to properly thank you for rescuing me."

"Rescuing you?"

"From the clutches of the rabid mob."

278

"What rabid mob?"

"The disappointed concertgoing mob."

Jesse didn't say anything.

They looked at each other for a long moment.

"I'm thinking vodka," she said.

"With tonic, right?"

She smiled at him.

He fixed the drink for her, then excused himself for a moment in order to go upstairs to turn off the TV.

She wandered into the living room.

From the dark corner of the porch, Rollo had witnessed Alexis's arrival. When Jesse left her alone in the living room, Rollo contemplated both his good fortune and how best to take advantage of it.

When she strolled to the French doors, opened them, and stepped outside, he knew that the voices had once again steered him correctly.

Alexis took a deep breath of sea air and gazed in the direction of the bay. The rising moon cast shadows on the landscape. She was happy to be here, she thought. She felt comfortable in Jesse's environment.

She was completely unprepared for the

ferocious attack that came from out of the dark.

A seeming giant of a man flew at her from the shadows. She lost her balance and fell awkwardly to the deck. The man jumped on top of her, knocking the wind out of her.

He straddled her legs with his, which prevented her from moving. Trying to catch her breath, she looked at his distorted face just in time to see him raise his fist and slam it heavily into her jaw. She fought to remain conscious but failed.

Rollo dragged her inside. He took a length of rope from his duffel and tied her arms behind her.

Then he went to the kitchen and picked up the pistol he had seen Jesse place on the counter.

He walked back to Alexis, took a can of lighter fluid from his bag, and emptied it on her.

Jesse heard a strange noise coming from downstairs, but he dismissed it when he realized that Alexis had probably gone onto the porch.

Still, he thought, *you can't be too careful.* Realizing he had left his pistol downstairs, he reached inside the bureau drawer for his backup, a Smith & Wesson automatic. He put it in his pocket and went downstairs.

The smell of lighter fluid greeted him as he entered the living room. Alexis was awkwardly slumped on one of his armchairs, her hands tied behind her. She appeared to be unconscious.

In the darkness behind her stood Rollo Nurse, the Colt Commander trained on Jesse.

"Jesse Stone," he said. "Remember me?"

Jesse didn't say anything.

"A lot of years. Too many to count. All of them spent in prison, dreaming of this moment," Rollo said. "I imagined every conceivable possibility, but this is a whole lot better than anything I could've thunk up."

"Tell me that when it's over," Jesse said.

"For you it's already over," Rollo said.

Alexis stirred. Her eyes fluttered open.

"Look at me, Stone," Rollo said. "Look at my face. This is what you did to me. This is how you left me. Now it's my turn."

Jesse watched as Alexis came fully awake. He saw her realize that her arms were bound. She smelled the lighter fluid. She became terrified.

Rollo stepped forward.

"Back up, Stone," he said to Jesse, gesturing with the Colt.

Jesse held his ground.

"Back up, I said."

Jesse took a step toward Rollo, who shied for an instant, then regained himself. With a wave of the gun, he again urged Jesse to step backward.

He took the throwaway lighter from his pocket. He flicked it into flame a couple of times to make certain it was working.

"Conflagration," he said to Jesse. "Death by fire. Just like in the Bible. You get to watch your girlfriend burn to death."

Rollo looked at Alexis, who was now wide awake.

"Nice of you to join us," he said. "It's much better to experience death with your eyes open, don't you think? Being awake so enriches the event. Stand up."

Alexis stared at him.

"I said stand up."

As if to emphasize his point, he flicked the lighter. He made certain she could see the flame. Reluctantly, she stood.

"She's not part of this, Rollo."

"Wrong, Stone. She is. So she dies. You get to watch."

Jesse had begun to inch closer to Rollo.

When he realized what Jesse was doing, Rollo fired the Colt in his direction. The bullet missed Jesse and slammed into the wall.

"Looking to be a hero, Stone," Rollo said. "Try that again and the girlfriend here will get to watch you die. Next time I won't miss."

Rollo began to nervously flick the lighter on and off.

"All those years," he said. "Alone in a cell. The best years of my life. Gone to hell. And the headaches. The sickness. All because of what you did to me, Stone. I can't remember things no more. You didn't have to hit me like that. You were drunk. You were out of control. And it was me paid the price."

Rollo took a step in Jesse's direction, waving the pistol at him.

"Now I'm out of control," he yelled at the top of his lungs. "Now it's you gonna pay the price."

He looked back at Alexis and approached her. He flicked the lighter, and it leapt into flame. He pointed it at her. She gasped and recoiled. He let it go out.

"Don't be scared, girlfriend," he said. "After the initial charring, you won't feel a thing."

With Rollo's attention focused on Alexis, Jesse turned slightly and placed his right hand in the pocket that held the Smith &

Wesson. He gripped it.

Rollo fired up the lighter again and this time, he held it closer to Alexis. He moved it toward her clothing. Just as he was about to touch it to her dress, he extinguished the flame.

Alexis screamed.

Rollo laughed.

He fired up the lighter again.

"Stop it," Jesse said.

When Rollo continued to ignore him, Jesse began to slowly withdraw the pistol from his pocket.

Rollo once again pointed the lighter in Alexis's direction.

She turned away from him.

He was near her, the flame inching closer and closer to her lighter-fluid-drenched clothing.

Suddenly she shifted her hips and kicked her left leg high in the air behind her. She caught Rollo full force in the throat.

He dropped the lighter and the pistol, and grabbed for his neck. Alexis knew she had delivered a lethal blow. She knew she had collapsed his windpipe.

There was terror in Rollo's eyes as he struggled for breath. How could this have happened? The voices were silent. He dropped to his knees.

He noticed the lighter on the floor beside him. Gasping for breath, he picked it up, flicked it into flame, and set Alexis on fire.

The pistol was out of Jesse's pocket. As soon as he saw Rollo extend the lighter, he fired.

The shot ripped into Rollo's head, shattering his skull, killing him instantly.

Alexis's clothing was ablaze. She was screaming.

Jesse leapt at her, knocking her to the ground. He fell on top of her, covering her with his body, attempting to smother the flames.

He ripped the smoldering clothes from her, leaving her naked and trembling on the floor. She moaned in pain.

He grabbed some ice packs from the refrigerator and placed them on her burns.

He reached for his cell phone and called the patrol car that was parked outside. He instructed them to immediately summon an ambulance.

He then untied her arms. He reached for the knitted afghan that was on one of the armchairs. He gently covered her with it.

He knelt down, lifted her up, and cradled her in his arms. She raised her head and looked at him.

"The ice packs are kind of kinky," she said.

He smiled at her. He held her until the medics knocked on his door.

Dr. Lifland had insisted that Alexis spend the night in the hospital. Although her burns proved not to be life threatening, they were burns nonetheless, and the doctor wanted to keep her under observation for at least twenty-four hours. He was concerned about the possibility of infection, as well as pain management.

Jesse sat in a bedside chair.

"Tell me again why you came to the house," he said.

"I was in a forgiving mood," she said.

"What if I wasn't," Jesse said.

"I was hoping what I had planned for you might change that."

"Which was?"

"The old roll-in-the-hay tactic."

"Oh, that," Jesse said.

"It's always worked before," she said.

"Am I that easy?"

"I couldn't say. I never got the chance to find out," Alexis said.

"But you did get to experience the exhilaration of lethal contact."

"Don't tease me, Jesse. He would have killed you. He was insane."

"I'm somewhat the cause of that," he said.

"What do you mean?"

"When I took him down in L.A., I brutalized him."

"And now you're holding yourself responsible for his death," she said.

"Maybe."

"He murdered Steve Lesnick. He set me on fire. He was going to kill you, Jesse."

Jesse didn't say anything.

"You can only do what you can do," Alexis said. "You can't take responsibility for everything."

"You think?"

"I know," she said.

"Tell me about the old roll in the hay again," he said.

"No."

"No?"

"The doctor told me not to get excited."

"What about tomorrow?"

"We'll cross that bridge when we come to it."

"We?"

"For now," she said, and closed her eyes.

59

Jesse had never thrown a party.

Daisy's had been hired to cater it. All of her servers were on hand to work it.

A bar had been set up on the front lawn, and one of Daisy's people was behind it, pouring drinks.

Two immense barbecues were across from the bar. Chicken, ribs, and burgers all sizzled over the hot coals. Massive trays of potato salad, coleslaw, and condiments stood at the ready.

A dessert bar offered different flavors of ice cream, as well as cupcakes, donuts, and pies. Platters of fresh fruit flanked the end of the table.

It was a glorious day. The weather couldn't have been more accommodating.

This is why we live in Paradise, Jesse thought.

The party was Jesse's way of saying thank you to everyone who had contributed to the restoration of his home.

It only seemed as if every resident of Paradise had shown up. Jesse made every effort to be a gracious host. Molly had come early and had been there to greet the guests and point them in the direction of the food and drink. Once things were running smoothly, she came over and stood beside Jesse.

"Nice," she said.

"Better than nice," Jesse said.

"Have you tried the shrimp thingies?"

"Not yet."

"Try them. I'm working on a scheme to squirrel dozens of them out of here without anyone noticing," she said.

"Good luck with that," Jesse said.

They stood, watching the crowd for a while.

"How's Alexis," she said.

"Good now. The bandages are off, and she appears to be healing nicely."

"Will she be here?"

"Doctor still wants her to rest."

"Too bad. How are you," she said.

"Better since I gave up hope."

"Haven't I heard that line before," she said.

"Are you suggesting that I'm repeating myself?"

"Whatever gave you that idea," she said.

Jesse didn't say anything.

"I hope you'll excuse me," Molly said. "I gotta go see a man about some shrimp."

She winked at him and made tracks for the food.

Jesse smiled.

The party was still going when it got dark. Jesse had grown tired of it.

He went inside to lie down, but the din of the party disturbed him. He phoned the station.

"Paradise Police Department," the voice answered.

Jesse recognized it as belonging to Rich Bauer.

"There's too much noise coming from the Jesse Stone party," Jesse said. "Can you send someone out to quiet things down?"

After a long moment, Bauer spoke.

"Jesse," he said. "Is this you?"

Grinning, Jesse hung up the phone.

60

The sky was heavy on the Fourth of July. Rain threatened, but as the day wore on, the threat diminished. The festival went on as planned.

People kept pouring into the stadium. By late afternoon, there were close to twelve hundred people watching and listening to the music. People of all ages were there. Teenagers experiencing their first daylong concert. Sixty-somethings reliving their youth. Lots of tweeners.

Dancing was de rigueur.

Business at the concession stands was booming. Beer and wine were selling briskly.

Alexis was in her element. Fully recovered, she kept the show going with the brisk efficiency of a field marshal. Her team had been well prepared, and the concert went off with military precision.

She spotted Jesse standing amid a group of his officers. She wandered over and pulled him aside.

"This is amazing," she said.

Jesse smiled.

"We even stand to make a fair sum of money. Uncle Carter is ecstatic."

"You've done a good job. You should be proud," Jesse said.

"Thank you, Jesse. Will I see you later?"

"Not likely. Suitcase is in charge. I'm gonna hang around a bit longer, then it's sayonara for me."

"I'll call you," she said.

She kissed his cheek and disappeared into the crowd.

Jesse strolled the grounds for a while. Summer was in full swing. The drama of spring was over. The tension had evaporated.

But at a price.

It was true he had set up John Lombardo. He had been aiming at him from the start. At the outset, he didn't know who he was, but he always knew what he was. He felt no remorse for what had occurred.

He thought about Rollo Nurse. He couldn't help but wonder whether he was responsible for all that Rollo had wrought. He recalled that night in L.A. Jesse was out of control, as Rollo had charged on the night that he died. Jesse had been drunk.

He had transferred his rage at Jenn onto Rollo. Which carried a heavy emotional price tag. Despite Rollo's death, Jesse knew he still wasn't finished paying it off.

He looked around at the crowd. They were content to share food and comfort and mutual respect in a friendly and peaceful environment.

Jesse was happy for Alexis. This was indeed her success. A big step up the ladder of her choosing. He knew that in short order she'd be gone, climbing still higher on that ladder.

His reverie was interrupted by Robert Lopresti, who was calling his name.

When Jesse turned, Lopresti pointed to a pretty young woman who was sitting on a blanket along with two small children. He waved for Jesse to join them.

"This is Angie," Lopresti said, introducing his wife to Jesse. "These are my children, Bobby Jr. and Lisette."

"Lisette?"

"I didn't get to choose her name," Robert said.

"You have a lovely family," Jesse said.

"I got the job," Robert said.

"I hope he's not making you intern."

"Nah. He's paying me. A good wage, too."

"Be sure to count it carefully," Jesse said.

"I aim to do you proud, Jesse."

"You already have."

They said their good-byes, and Jesse found his way out of the stadium. He got into his cruiser and drove away.

It was still light when he got home.

He cracked a beer and strolled onto the porch. He sat down on the new love seat. He took a long pull on the beer, then nestled deep into the luxuriously comfortable pillows.

Mildred Memory poked her head through the rubber veil at the bottom of the door. She stepped out and padded her way to the love seat. She jumped onto Jesse's lap.

She turned around a couple of times, then, after repeatedly rubbing her chin against Jesse's cheek, she settled down and began to purr.

Jesse took another sip of beer.

He gently scratched Mildred Memory's neck.

She looked up at him, sleepy-eyed.

He smiled at her.

ACKNOWLEDGMENTS

The author wishes to thank Joanna Miles, Melanie Mintz, Kim Kimball Holmquist, and Miles Brandman for their invaluable assistance in the development of this book.

Thanks also to Tom Distler for his wise and temperate counsel.

Thanks to David Parker and Daniel T. Parker.

A world of gratitude to Tom Selleck and the entire Jesse Stone movie universe for their inspiration and support.

A special thanks to Christine C. Pepe for her kindness, patience, and incredible editorial expertise.

The spirit, guidance, and generosity of Joan Parker meant the world to me.

And a special nod to Helen Brann, who grabbed my hand and never let go until we crossed the finish line.

ABOUT THE AUTHORS

Robert B. Parker was the author of seventy books, including the legendary Spenser detective series, the novels featuring Chief Jesse Stone, and the acclaimed Virgil Cole/ Everett Hitch westerns, as well as the Sunny Randall novels. Winner of the Mystery Writers of America Grand Master Award and long considered the undisputed dean of American crime fiction, he died in January 2010.

Michael Brandman, the award-winning producer of more than thirty motion pictures, collaborated with Robert B. Parker for years on movie projects, the Spenser TV movies, and the Jesse Stone series of TV movies starring Tom Selleck. Brandman cowrote the screenplays for *Stone Cold, No Remorse,* and *Innocents Lost,* and supervised the screenplay adaptions of *Night Passage, Death in Paradise,* and *Sea Change.* He and

Selleck were executive producers of the entire series. Brandman lives in California.